The Ghost Therapists

A Tess and Tilly Mystery

by

Kathi Daley

Tess and Tilly Cozy Mystery

The Christmas Letter

The Valentine Mystery

The Mother's Day Mishap

The Halloween House

The Thanksgiving Trip

The Saint Paddy's Promise

The Halloween Haunting

The Christmas Clause

The Puppy Project

The Wedding Plan

The Baby Plan

The Ghostly Groundskeeper

The Murder Chronicles

The Castle Caper

The Christmas Visitor

The Sleuthing Game

The Ghost Therapists

Chapter 1

"The Ghost Therapists, Tim Rivers and Tom Masters, have dedicated their lives to helping lost souls tethered to this earthly plain deal with their unfinished business in the hope they will finally be able to move on," drawled Laura Lane, the anchorwoman who'd been assigned to interview Tony and me about the upcoming *Ghost Therapy* special that would be filmed in our hometown of White Eagle, Montana. "Tim and Tom were unable to be here today," she continued to speak into the camera, "so event organizers, Tess and Tony Marconi, are filling in." The woman turned away from the camera and looked toward Tony and me. "Thank you for being here today," the woman said as she looked directly at my enlarged stomach, "although, given your condition, I'm sure it would have been fine to send Tony on his own."

"Of course, but I wanted to be here," I said in a tolerant tone, even though I was well aware that her objection to my presence had more to do with how things looked than how I felt. "Kiwi and I wouldn't miss it." I looked down and gave my stomach a rub.

The woman, who I was sure had no children of her own given her obvious discomfort with my state of impending motherhood, gave me the oddest look before she recovered and asked her first question, which she directed toward Tony. "Mr. Marconi, I understand that rather than focusing on a single haunted house as Tim and Tom have chosen to do in the past, the men plan to counsel multiple ghosts."

Tony smiled and nodded. "Yes, that does seem to be their most recent plan. I don't have all the details, but I've been told that the men have identified three targets in addition to the Stonewall Estate. All four *Ghost Therapy* episodes will be filmed during the same week. The first three episodes will be filmed without audience participation. The fourth and final ghostly therapy session will be a much longer segment to be filmed at the Stonewall Estate."

"And will an auction be held for tickets for audience participation like the last time the men were in town?" Laura asked.

This time, I jumped in with an answer. "Yes, Laura, there will be an auction for participation during the session at the Stonewall Estate. The winning bids will be announced at the end of this week." I looked directly into the camera and smiled. "I'd like to remind your viewers that all proceeds from the auction will go to the town for special programs such as our animal rescue center, volunteer firefighters, and free library."

"There will also be a lottery for White Eagle residents," Tony jumped back in. "Ten names will be chosen, and the winners will receive an invite free of charge."

Laura looked back toward the camera. "So there you have it, folks. It looks as if the town of White Eagle has plans to clear out all its ghostly residents in a single week. If you have deep pockets and have always wanted to sit in on a ghost therapy session, the website that will take you to the auction is on the monitor."

Someone yelled cut, and Laura put her microphone down.

"Is that it?" I asked. "Did Tony and I come all the way to Billings for a sixty second interview?"

She shrugged. "As far as I'm concerned, you were lucky to get that. Personally, I thought it was a mistake to give any level of legitimacy to the quacks who claim to help lost souls move on. But the station manager felt it would be a fun interview to throw into the mix with Halloween just around the corner, so he agreed to the request from your mayor to include it."

"What Tim and Tom do might be unconventional, but I wouldn't really call them quacks." I defended the men, who I thought were quite pleasant the last time Tony and I worked with them.

She raised a brow. "Really? Surely you don't believe all this ghost stuff."

"Well, I can't say with any degree of certainty that ghosts actually exist, but I have seen some things in my day that suggest that there's at least a possibility that they do." I took a breath and then continued. "Tim and Tom are well-known ghost therapists. They aren't just backyard enthusiasts. They have a nationally syndicated show that's really quite popular."

"So I've heard." She adjusted her hair with one hand. "I have to go. Things to do and all that. It was nice to meet you." She glanced at my very handsome husband and smiled. "Both of you."

What a b.... I stopped myself before I even finished the thought. I was going to be a mother. I knew I'd need to set an example for Kiwi, and even though she wasn't yet born, I knew I needed to begin cultivating some level of decorum.

"I suppose it went as well as one could have expected," Tony said.

"Did it?"

"It was a bit briefer than I'd anticipated, but I think we got the message out there that we wanted to deliver."

"I guess."

"How about we have lunch before we head back to the airport. I didn't arrange for the plane to pick us up for the trip back to White Eagle until three o'clock since I wasn't exactly sure how long the interview would take."

I slipped my hand into Tony's. "Lunch sounds good. I have a message from Bree, which I'll return on the drive to the restaurant."

Bree Thomas was married to my brother, Mike Thomas. They were expecting a baby any day, and it seemed that the closer Bree got to her delivery date, the more times a day she called me. She was so excited that we were having babies within two months of one another, but neither baby was born yet, so I didn't think decisions such as which preschool our children would attend together were all that urgent.

Once we'd settled into the rental car, Tony headed toward the restaurant near the airport we'd agreed on, and I called my best friend and sister-in-law. "Hey, Bree. What's up?"

"I had my doctor's appointment today, and she said Michael should be here any day now. Can you believe everything actually might be on schedule this time around?"

"I'm really happy for you. I'm sure you're more than ready to deliver at this point."

"I am. And Mike is ready for me to deliver as well. Apparently, the closer I get to my due date, the more emotional I become. Personally I think that Mike's the one who's gotten all emotional lately, but you know your brother. You can't tell him anything."

I did know my brother, but I also knew Bree, and she did tend to have significant mood swings at most stages of her pregnancies. Mike had been doing a good job keeping his cool despite the emotional rollercoaster he'd been living on for the last nine months, but I was sure both Mike and Bree were ready for a level of sanity to return to the Thomas household.

"Your father stopped by earlier," Bree said, segueing into, I suspected, the real reason for her call. "I know he wants to be here for all the important moments in Michael's life since he missed so much when Ella was born, but I find it disconcerting to come down for my morning tea to find him sitting at my kitchen table."

My father, Grant Thomas, aka Grant Tucker, aka Walton Davis, aka a bunch of other aliases, died in a fiery crash years ago, although, I would later learn that his death had been faked as part of his attempt to disappear and protect his family. My father had spent his life deeply integrated into a black ops arm of the CIA. After being shot and almost dying in the line of duty and finding it necessary to recoup with Tony and me this past holiday season, he'd finally decided it was time to retire and get to know his family. The transition wasn't easy since he needed to establish a new identity, but he'd been working on it. Not only would he have a new name and history before he went public, but he'd already had facial reconstruction that had turned out quite nice if you asked me.

"I think you and Mike need to set some boundaries with Dad now that he's bought that land up on the mountain and plans to build a cabin there," I suggested. "If you don't, your life won't be your own."

"Have you and Tony set boundaries with your father?" she asked.

"No," I admitted. "Dad still drops in whenever it suits him. Initially, his visits were brief and infrequent, so I didn't mind the random visits, but I heard he's moved a trailer up to his property on the river, which he plans to live in until his cabin is built. Recovery from his surgery is just about complete, so I suspect the new man in town, whose name has yet to be revealed, will likely show up any day now."

"And there will be nothing to stop him from being a real pest once he decides to go public with his new identity if we don't establish and enforce some rules," Bree said.

"I agree. Tony and I are heading into a restaurant for lunch before our flight back to White Eagle, so I'll call you later. Maybe the four of us should get together and decide how best to handle the situation without hurting Dad's feelings."

"Yeah," Bree sighed. "Okay. Call me when you get home."

With that, I hung up and turned to look at Tony. "I think my dad is beginning to outstay his welcome with Bree."

"I heard. I know that your father is used to popping in whenever he's in town, and I know he's trying to make up for lost time, but I agree that we might want to set some boundaries before things get out of hand." Tony pulled into a parking spot and turned the car off. "I hope this restaurant is as good as

I remember it being the last time I was here. I'm starving."

"We didn't have much for breakfast, and the lunch hour has come and gone. I could go for a club sandwich and fries if they have them on the menu."

Tony smiled and took my hand in his. "You seem to be all about the fries since you've been pregnant."

I shrugged. "I guess Kiwi knows what she likes."

Tony and I had yet to settle on a name for our baby girl, so we'd been calling her Kiwi, the name we began using early on when we were told our baby was the size of a kiwi. Our little angel had grown since then and, more often than not, liked to camp out on my bladder. Like Bree, I would be happy when my baby was born, and I'd finally be able to reclaim my body.

Tony requested a table for two near the window. Once we were seated, I looked over the menu while he pulled his cell phone out and checked his messages. I was pretty sure I knew what I wanted, but it never hurt to glance at the menu, especially at a new eatery. Since Tony had previously eaten at this restaurant, he knew what he wanted to order.

"I have a text from Jasmine," Tony informed me. Jasmine Shaw was the new producer for *Ghost Therapy*. She'd come on after the original producer had decided to move out of the country six months ago.

"And what does Jazzy want?"

"She texted to let me know that Tim and Tom have finalized the lineup for next week. Jazzy has a crew lined up, and she assures me that she has signed contracts with the owner of each property the men plan to use for filming. She shared that she feels ready but hoped I could view each property to look for obstacles that might need to be addressed before taping. She asked that I walk around and take some photos to provide the men an idea of what to expect when they arrive."

I set my menu down and shrugged. "That sounds easy enough. Maybe you and I can drive to the four locations tomorrow and check them out."

"I'll make some calls when we get home to arrange it," Tony said.

"Which sites did the men settle on besides the Stonewall Estate?"

"They plan to start with the old movie theater on Monday."

"The old theater on the highway south of town?"

Tony confirmed this was indeed the facility the men had chosen.

I knew the property. "That building has been abandoned for years. Decades, in fact. I don't remember exactly when the establishment ceased operations, but the theater permanently shut down during my early childhood. Are you telling me there's a ghost living there?"

Tony shrugged. "I really have no idea if a spirit haunts the property, but Tim and Tom seem to have reason to believe that the ghost of Gavigan O'Leary still roams the halls."

"And who is Gavigan O'Leary?" I asked.

"He was an usher at the old theater during its heyday. He was responsible for opening and closing the place and frequently helped in the snack bar."

"He died on the property?"

Tony nodded, glancing down at his cell phone, "He was stabbed twelve times, and his body was found behind the curtain in nineteen ninety-five."

Now that Tony said that, I remembered hearing something about a murder on the property. In fact, I seemed to remember there being talk that the stabbing might not have been personal but opportunistic in nature. The movie showing at the theater the week the man died was a slasher movie, and the number and pattern of stab wounds found on his body exactly mimicked the number and pattern delivered by the killer in that movie.

"I take it the case was never solved, and Tim and Tom think Gavigan O'Leary's spirit has been trapped in that old theater all this time."

"That does seem to be the premise for the therapy session. Apparently, the knife used to kill the man was never found, and without fingerprints to run, the police never could come up with any real clues."

"It seems to me that if the unfinished business keeping the man's spirit trapped in the movie theater is the inability of the police to solve the murder, then

Tim and Tom, or someone, might need to solve the case before Gavigan can move on."

"I don't disagree with that, but I suspect that Tim and Tom simply hope to contact the man and find out why he's sticking around."

"The murder occurred almost thirty years ago. If the man has been waiting for someone to finally put all the pieces of this puzzle together, he may never experience closure."

"I don't disagree with that either," Tony said.

The waiter came to take our order, pausing the conversation. When the waiter left to deliver our order to the kitchen, I asked Tony about the other ghosts the Ghost Therapists planned to try to help.

"Tim and Tom will visit with Nancy Whelan on Wednesday. Nancy owns an antique shop in Kalispell. I guess Nancy purchased a chest of drawers, which she feels certain is haunted by the ghost of one of its previous owners."

"A chest of drawers?" I asked. "So this ghost isn't bound to a building or other physical location but rather to an object."

"That seems to be the case."

I wrinkled my nose. "I'm willing to suspend disbelief in the spirit of Halloween and all its ghostly traditions, but that seems a bit too far-fetched for me."

Tony took a sip of his water. "I agree, but it should be entertaining."

I supposed Tony had a point.

"And on Friday?" I asked.

"Friday will be dedicated to counseling the ghost of Beatrice Montrose. I guess Beatrice died in her home three years ago, and her sister, Hannah, feels certain that she still walks the hallways of the lakefront mansion they inherited from their father."

"Was Beatrice murdered?"

Tony shook his head. "She died in her sleep. As far as I know, a cause of death was never specified, but foul play was not suspected. Since she was an older woman, the cause of death was just listed as natural on the death certificate."

"So where is the unfinished business?" I asked.

Tony lifted a shoulder. "I really don't have all the details. I imagine Tim and Tom will fill us in once they arrive on Saturday."

"So they will be here two days before the first therapy session."

"That's my understanding. In addition to preparing for the three private sessions, the men will need to prepare for the live audience gig at the Stonewall Estate. The Stonewall thing, as you know, is an after-dark event, so I doubt they'll have the audience show up until late in the afternoon on Saturday."

I was uncertain whether managing four events in one week was advisable. But since it wasn't my show and my opinion hadn't been asked, I decided to keep my feelings to myself and support Tony as he acted as the local liaison to the men who might not be as connected to the ghostly realm as they liked everyone to believe but somehow still seemed to put on a heck of an entertaining show.

Chapter 2

Once we returned home from Billings, I took the dogs out onto the deck so they could run around and get some fresh air while Tony made the calls he needed to make to set things up for our tour of haunted objects and places the following day. The attorney who managed the land where the theater was located had left a set of keys with a real estate agent he'd previously worked with. We decided we'd stop by and pick the keys up and then do a walkthrough of the theater immediately after.

Nancy Whelan, who owned an antique shop Tim and Tom planned to visit on Wednesday, was in Kalispell, so we decided to go there second. Nancy suggested we come by around lunchtime, when she traditionally closed the store for an hour, so she could tell us the entire story of the chest of drawers without interruption.

Once we finished in Kalispell, we planned to head to the estate owned by Hannah Dunningham to speak to her about the possible haunting of the family estate by her sister, Beatrice Montrose, who had never married. It looked as if the day would be long, but the fatigue I'd been feeling early in my pregnancy seemed to have diminished, so I figured Kiwi and I would be okay.

"I think we should bring Tilly with us tomorrow," I said to Tony after he joined me on the deck. "She seems to have developed a bit of separation anxiety lately, and I'm pretty sure she isn't going to want to be left home alone all day tomorrow after having been left home alone all day today."

Tony frowned. "I feel bad about leaving any of the animals home for two consecutive days. We'll take Tilly with us, but I think I'll ask Shaggy if he can work from our house tomorrow."

Shaggy was Tony's best friend and his business partner. While Tony made the majority of his fortune developing security software, Shaggy had come to him with an idea for a video game that had sold so well that the men immediately began to work on a second and then a third game.

"I'm sure Titan and Kody will enjoy having company." Titan was Tony's rescue dog, and Kody was my search and rescue dog. I supposed our cats wouldn't care one way or the other, but I would feel better with Shaggy and his dog, Buddy, on the premises.

"I'll call him," Tony said. "He mentioned needing to use some of my equipment at this point anyway, so it may work out for all of us as long as he has someone to cover the store."

Shaggy owned a video game store.

Tony called Shaggy, who was happy to have a full day in Tony's computer lab, and I called Mike, who had left several messages on my cell phone while it was on airplane mode. We'd been back in White Eagle for almost two hours, but I'd forgotten to turn my cell phone back on when we'd landed and hadn't even checked my cell phone until this very moment.

"It's Tess. I noticed five messages from you that I have yet to listen to. What's going on?" I asked after Mike answered.

"Bree started having fairly intense contractions a few hours ago, so we headed to the hospital. When it looked like they planned to admit her, she asked me to call you. But her contractions have stopped completely in the past forty minutes or so, and now they're talking about sending her home. You might as well wait to come into town until I call you back. If Bree is sent home, there's no point in you driving all the way into town."

"We had a long day, and I am pretty tired, so if Bree is sent home, I would prefer to save myself the trip. Of course, if it's 'go time,' I'll power through and be there for her every step of the way."

"The doctor's talking to her now, so I'll call you back when I know more. How did your interview go?"

"It was brief but fine. Tony and I have plans to go out tomorrow and preview all three locations the men plan to use as a warmup to the big event at the Stonewall Estate. Did you hear that one of the haunted places is actually a chest of drawers and not a building?"

"I hadn't heard. How does that work?"

"I guess the ghost is attached to the furniture and moves with it when it moves."

"Seems unlikely."

"I don't disagree with that, but seeing what Tim and Tom do with the whole thing should be interesting."

"Listen, I need to go. Bree is texting me to come back to the room. I'll call you once I find out what's going on."

I clicked my cell phone off and then looked up as Tony came out onto the deck with two of the alcohol-free mocktails he'd been making for us each evening since I'd found out I was pregnant.

"Was that Mike?" he asked.

"It was. Bree may or may not be having the baby today." I explained the situation. "He's going to call me back after he talks to Bree." I held up my glass. "I love the orange color. Very fallish. What is it?"

"I used apple cider for a base and then added a bit of apricot, sparkling cider, and some spices. The whole thing is topped off with a sprinkling of my own secret ingredients. I wasn't sure how it would come out, but I tried a sip before I poured it, and I think it's both delicious and refreshing."

I took a sip. "It is good. Is that mint I taste?"

He nodded. "I did add fresh mint, amongst other things." Tony set his glass on the table. "I received a call from my cousin in Italy while I was inside making the drinks."

"Is everything okay?" Tony had family in Italy, but they didn't often call.

"Everything's fine. Joseph just wanted to check in with me. He asked if we planned to visit in November, as we have a few times, but I told him that since you would be eight months pregnant by November, we wouldn't make the trip this year. He asked about the baby and her name. I told him we hadn't settled on a name, but the conversation got me thinking specifically about Italian names." He turned a bit so that he was looking directly at me. "What do you think of Antonella?"

"Antonella?" I asked.

"Antonella was Nona's birth name. I know it's a mouth full, but I thought it might be nice to honor the woman who made such a huge difference in my life by naming a daughter after her."

I paused to think about this for a moment. "The idea of naming our baby after Nona is lovely, but, as you've already said, Antonella seems too big for such a tiny little girl. Maybe we can come up with a nickname. You were named Anthony after Nona, but everyone calls you Tony. I truly like Toni for a girl, but that might be confusing."

"I agree that a nickname would be a good idea," Tony said. "In addition to Toni, which I agree would be confusing, Ella seems like a natural nickname, but we already have an Ella in the family. Maybe Nella or Stella or even just Anna or Annie."

"I don't hate any of those names, but they don't feel quite right either."

"Maybe we can play off Kiwi's middle name. Have you thought at all about that?" Tony asked.

"No. I've been focused on a first name to this point." I paused to consider the idea of a middle name. "My mother's name is Lucinda Theresa, and, as you know, she goes by Lucy. I was named after her, and like her middle name, my first name is Theresa, but as you know, I've always gone by Tess. After saying all that, I have considered the idea of Kiwi's middle name being Theresa after Mom and me."

"Antonella Theresa Marconi has an Italian feel to it."

I smiled. "It does, doesn't it?"

My cell phone rang. "Hey, Mike. What's the verdict?"

"They're going to send her home. The doctor seems to think we might have a couple more days, but she also said things should go fairly quickly once her labor starts. I guess the only thing we can do is to be on standby at this point."

"Okay. Tell Bree I love her, and I'll call her tomorrow."

I filled Tony in after I hung up. He suggested we have an early night since the possibility did exist that we could get called to the hospital in the middle of the night if the contractions started back again. I knew Bree was really anxious to have this baby, but personally, I was hoping for a daytime baby whose arrival wouldn't interrupt my sleep.

Chapter 3

I slept soundly and awoke feeling refreshed. A quick glance out the window confirmed the steady rain I thought I'd heard in the middle of the night. Sliding my legs out from under the thick quilts I'd stacked one atop another, I sat up on the side of the bed. Tilly, who'd been lying on the floor beside my bed, thumped her tail on the carpet. I smiled at her as I stood up and put my robe on.

"It looks like it's going to be a drizzly day," I told my best doggy friend. The sky was dark, and the landscape was wet with the moisture that had fallen overnight. "I guess we could use the rain," I said aloud as I stared out the window at the lush landscape.

Tilly seemed more interested in going out than in discussing the weather, as evidenced by the paw on my thigh, so I headed downstairs and let her out into the yard at the back of the house, where the kitchen was located.

"Oh good, you're awake," Tony said after I entered the kitchen, which was nice and toasty warm from the flames of the gas fireplace. "I'm preheating the oven for the biscuits. Breakfast will be ready in about fifteen minutes. Would you like some tea?"

"I would. I need to call Mike to find out how Bree is doing before I get distracted and forget. I let Tilly out, but given the rain, I suspect she'll be ready to come in sooner rather than later."

"I'll listen for her while you make your call."

I smiled at Tony as I reached down to pet Titan and Kody. Both had come over to say hi before I called my brother, who informed me that Bree's contractions had stopped completely and that she was resting comfortably, although her mental state wasn't the best. He also shared that Mom and Sam had offered to take Ella for a few days while Bree dealt with her labor, or lack of labor, as the case might be. I was tempted to stop by and check in on Bree, but Tony and I already had a long day ahead of us, so after I spoke to Mike, who was already in his office, I called Bree and offered to come by later if we didn't get home too late.

Bree was understandably feeling down about the fact that Michael hadn't arrived last night as she'd hoped, but she admitted that she felt okay today and would probably work on the blanket she'd been knitting for Michael the last time I'd stopped by for a chat. Bree tended to engage in a hobby or craft of one kind or another when she was feeling stressed, which meant that Ella and Michael each had at least ten handmade blankets by this point.

When I returned to the kitchen, Tilly was drying off next to the fireplace, and both cats were curled up next to her.

"How's Bree?" Tony asked.

"Frustrated but otherwise okay. Bree still has a week until her due date, but she seems ready to have things over with."

"I guess I can't blame her for that."

I sat on one of the chairs near the large window that looked out over the backyard and our private lake. The muddy walkway out to the lake suggested that there had been a significant amount of rain since Tony and I had gone to bed last evening.

"It's so cozy in here with the rain and the fire that I sort of hate to have to leave," I said as Tony set a cup of gynecologist-approved herbal tea in front of me.

"I can do the tour alone if you want to stay home," Tony offered.

"If you leave, it won't be cozy any longer. Tilly and I will go as we planned to. What time is Shaggy coming over?"

"Shaggy wanted to stop by the store and check in with his staff before he headed up the mountain, so he'll be here around eleven," Tony informed me as he poured eggs he'd already beaten into a pan. "He has a key, so he can let himself in. I'll take Titan and Kody out for a bathroom break before we head out, so they should be fine until he gets here. The cats are fed, have fresh water, litter boxes are cleaned, and once we eat and I take the dogs out, I think we should be ready to go."

"Did you arrange a specific time to pick up the key the attorney overseeing the theater property left with the real estate agent?"

"Not a specific time. I did say we'd likely be by around nine or nine-thirty, and the woman was fine with that. She told me to talk to Susan if she wasn't in when we arrived. Susan's been apprised of what's happening and can get us what we need."

Tony set a basket of hot from the oven biscuits on the table, along with a jar of huckleberry jam he'd made late in the season last year.

"I know the old theater is in a state of disrepair and that most folks in town feel it needs to come down, but if they tear down the old place, it will be so weird not to see it there any longer. It was built in the nineteen fifties. Not that I was around back then to know the difference, but when I was around five or six, my dad took me there to see a movie."

"Mike and your mom didn't go?" Tony asked as he set a plate of scrambled eggs and fresh fruit on the table for me.

"No. It was Christmas, or at least shortly before Christmas. My dad was home and didn't have another run until after New Year's Day, so he offered to entertain Mike and me so Mom could finish her shopping and do some baking. Mike wanted to hang out with his friends, so Dad dropped him off and took me to a movie." I paused to think back to that incredibly significant day. "I was pretty young and don't remember much about it, but I do remember feeling special since my dad rarely took the time to spend one-on-one time with me. He occasionally took Mike out for the day, but I don't think he knew what to do with a girl."

"Do you remember what movie you saw?" Tony asked.

I shook my head. "No idea. It was a kids' Christmas movie of one sort or another. I'm pretty sure my dad was bored out of his mind, but he didn't let it show. He was actually very attentive. He bought me a soda and some candy, and he even talked to me about the movie during the drive to pick Mike up from his friend's house."

"The theater wasn't abandoned until two thousand four," Tony said. "I guess you must have attended other movies there."

"No. At least not that I remember. Neither of my parents liked to go out to the movies, so other than that one time with my dad, I don't remember either of them taking me to one. Mike is older than I am, so he might have been old enough to go with friends before the old theater closed, but my parents were pretty strict with me. When I was around nine or ten, I remember that they built the new theater in town and that the old place on the highway began a rapid downhill decline. I don't remember the exact dates off hand, but the new theater in town was already open, and the old place on the highway was closed by the time I was old enough to go to the movies without parental supervision."

After finishing my meal, I pushed my plate to the center of the table.

"I'm going to clean up and then take the dogs out," Tony informed me.

"I'm going to head upstairs to get ready."

Once I'd washed up and changed into the clothes I planned to wear that day, I grabbed my purse, sweater, and raincoat, which I was sure wouldn't zip up in front but would still offer a degree of protection from the rain, and headed toward the staircase. As I walked past the nursery, which was completely outfitted and ready for Kiwi's arrival, even though she wasn't due to make her grand entry into the world for another two months, I paused briefly before stepping inside. We'd decided on a storybook theme, which featured a lot of different colors and patterns. My favorite item was the storybook quilt my mom had made. Each center square had been stitched with a different storybook theme, which must have taken days and days to complete. The base colors in the room were dark red and dark gold, which felt welcoming and gender-neutral should we decide to repurpose some of the newborn pieces for baby number two when he or she came along.

Walking over to the crib, I ran a hand over the headboard. I often came into the room and tried to imagine what it would be like to watch my baby sleep in the presently empty space. I couldn't know what she would look like, of course, but Tony and I both had brown hair and brown eyes, so I imagined that much at least would hold true. At this point, the small details, such as if her cheeks would be thin or full or if she'd be tall like Tony or short like me, eluded me.

"Antonella," I said aloud, letting the name settle in my mind. While I loved Tony's desire to name the baby after the woman who had played such a significant role in his childhood, I truly wanted a shorter name for everyday use.

My thoughts returned to the nicknames Tony and I had tossed around yesterday, but none were really jelling. We'd mentioned numerous names, and Toni definitely stood out as my favorite, but having both a 'Tony' and a 'Toni' under one roof would be much too confusing.

"Don't worry, baby. Mommy and Daddy will find the perfect name for you. I promise."

Tony called out from the bottom of the stairs, and I headed in that direction. We chatted about nothing and everything on our way into town, although I was preoccupied most of the time. The responsibility of selecting the perfect name for our little darling had weighed heavily on my mind for months. Tony didn't seem as worried about it as I was, but with my delivery date less than two months away, I felt pressured to come up with something.

Tony parked on the street in front of the real estate office. It had started to rain again, so he offered to run in and pick up the key while Tilly and I stayed warm and dry in the truck's cab. When Tony returned, he informed me that the real estate agent the attorney had left the key with wasn't in yet, but as promised, Susan had the key ready to hand off.

The property was located about five miles beyond the town limit and at least four miles from the nearest building. I wasn't sure why the theater had been built so far out of the way back in the fifties, but I supposed that land out this far was much less expensive than land closer to town and between the building and the large parking area it really did take up quite a bit of acreage. The old cement building was in disrepair and crumbling after decades of neglect, so tearing it down seemed to make sense. It was surrounded by tall weeds that grew on an equally tall fence with a gate. Tony had been given the key for the gate and the building, which was further padlocked with a heavy lock and rusted chain.

"It looks like someone really wanted to keep people out," I said as Tony fiddled with the lock.

"I guess they had a problem with kids breaking into the place to party and vagrants breaking in to escape the elements, so they stepped up security at some point. Not that this chain and padlock would deter anyone who truly wanted to get inside, but combined with the gate and door locks, it likely works on the causal teenager out to make trouble."

Once the door was open, Tony, Tilly, and I headed inside.

"Heel," I told Tilly to ensure she stayed close to me, where she would be less likely to get hurt in the dilapidated building.

Tilly was used to walking inches from my knee, which she did now.

"This is a lot freakier than I imagined it would be," I said as we entered the lobby, where the counter for the snack bar still stood.

"The candy display case and the old popcorn machine are still here," Tony said. "I guess I thought someone would have cleared it out by now."

"It looks like they simply packed up the food and candy, closed up, went home, and never returned." Given the multiple obstacles scattered across the floor, it was necessary to walk slowly and carefully so as not to trip on any of them.

"I have a feeling that Tim and Tom's fans are going to eat this up," Tony said. "The place is authentically creepy. I doubt the crew will even need to bring props to provide the chill factor the show is known for." Tony walked around the room, took some photos, and then headed toward a hallway that led to restrooms and the main body of the theater.

As predicted, the theater was outfitted with rows and rows of theater seating. The stage looked like any other theater stage, but the screen, which hung down at an angle, had been tagged with paint of different colors. I glanced around the room to find paint on the walls as well.

"It looks like there have been at least a few break-ins in the past thirty years," I said.

"I'm actually surprised the place isn't in worse shape than it is," Tony said.

"Why has this building been vacant for thirty years?" I asked. "I get that the theater in town opened, and since this theater was so far out of the way and there were closer options, business all but died, but this must have been a decent building thirty years ago. It's built on a large piece of land with plenty of parking. Even if the movie theater went belly up, it still seems like the land it occupied would likely have sold for a considerable amount of money."

"The story I heard was that one of the rich cattle barons in the area built the theater and then left it to his son. I can't remember which cattle baron built the place, but apparently, the man who owned the theater passed away only a few years after the theater went out of business. The building and the land it was built on were thrown into probate along with the rest of the estate. I guess things were messy, and the building and the land ended up in probate limbo. As far as I know, the estate is still unsettled, but as we have discussed, there has been a push from a group in town to tear down the building that many feel has become a dangerous lure for kids and vagrants."

"The building is in total disrepair," I agreed. "Tearing it down makes a lot of sense, but I will admit that I'm going to miss it and the spooky stories that came along with it if the group from town is successful."

"There have been some fun ghost stories about the place over the years," Tony said. "It seems odd to me that the actual ghost story involving the usher who had been stabbed twelve times never made the rounds."

"Maybe it did, but you don't remember, or maybe by the time we were old enough to start hearing the stories, it had changed like stories tend to do."

"There was that ghost story about the man with the machete and the group of teens who decided to spend the night in the place and were never seen again, but I'm pretty sure the whole thing was fiction."

Tony stopped walking about halfway down the aisle. Standing in the middle of the large room, he turned slowly in a circle. The stage and screen were located at the front of the building, and three aisles and four sections of seating were in the center of the structure. The projector room was at the back of the building. I was curious if anyone had left a movie behind since everything else seemed to have been left where it was when the last employee left on the final day the place was open.

"I suspect that if Tim and Tom are careful with the lighting, this old place will make for an excellent ghost encounter," I said.

"I agree. There's just enough natural eeriness to sell the idea of a ghost, and with all the dust and cobwebs, there won't be a need for any enhancement."

I looked down at my side to find it dogless. "Tilly," I called out. I'd been so enthralled by the interior of the movie theater that I hadn't even noticed that she'd wandered off.

"Tilly," Tony called in an even louder voice.

I heard her bark from somewhere off in the distance. It sounded as if the sound was coming from behind the screen.

"I'm going to go and get her," I said.

"I'll get her," Tony said. "There isn't adequate lighting in here, and I wouldn't want you tripping on anything."

Tony was right about it being a hazard to walk around. Between the lack of light and the obstacles littering the floor, the place was a minefield, and the last thing I wanted to do was hurt Kiwi. I was tempted to go for Tilly, but in the end, I merely agreed with Tony's plan and stayed where I was.

Of course, when neither Tony nor Tilly returned right away, I began to worry. "Tony," I called out. "Is everything okay?"

"I'm fine," he called back. "Tilly is fine as well. Hang on. We're making our way back to you."

I could tell by the look on Tony's face that while he might be fine, everything most definitely wasn't. "What is it?" I asked as I bent down to greet Tilly, who'd returned with Tony.

"I'm afraid Gavigan O'Leary isn't the only casualty of the theater."

"You found another body?"

"Tilly found another body. There's a room behind the screen. It's a small room designed to accommodate the control panels for the lighting and sound systems. The door was locked, but Tilly seemed insistent about getting in, so I tried the key to the theater that I was given this morning, and it worked. I'm afraid I found more than controls behind the door."

"Who?" I asked.

Tony shrugged. "Whoever it is has been dead for a while. There's no way to identify the body based on facial features. I called Mike before returning to you, and he's on his way. He suggested that we wait outside in the truck."

"Yeah," I said. "That sounds like a good idea."

Tony took my hand, I called Tilly, and the three of us headed back toward the lobby and the front door. Unfortunately, it was raining again, but I really wanted to reach the truck's safety, so I pulled the hood of my currently much too-small raincoat over my head and made a dash for the vehicle. After Tony loaded Tilly and me into the truck, he went around and climbed in on the driver's side.

"When Mike gets here, I'm going to take him inside and show him where Tilly found the body," Tony said. "You and Tilly should wait here."

"Okay," I agreed. "Do you think the body in the control room belongs to someone we know?"

"I hope not, but I really have no idea."

"How long do you think it's been there?"

"Again, I really have no idea. The body itself, at least the parts I could see, has almost completely decomposed, leaving little more than a skeleton. It appears like rodents have chewed the clothing, but it's still mostly intact. It's hard to say for certain if the remains belonged to a male or female, but the jeans, t-shirt, and flannel shirt over the t-shirt suggest a male victim. If I had to guess, the body has been there at least several months, but probably a year or longer. I'm really not an expert on such things, so I guess an estimate as to when the victim died is a question best asked of the coroner."

I looked out the window at the rain as it pelted the windshield. I supposed that if the body in the control room had been there for months or even years, someone must have reported them as missing. Tony had said there had been break-ins in the past, and the trash on the floor and graffiti on the walls seemed to support that, so I supposed our victim might have been a transient. At this point, I planned to wait to see what Mike said before I started worrying that the skeleton in the control room had been a friend or neighbor.

Mike and his partner, Frank, showed up a few minutes later, so Tony climbed out of the truck to escort them inside. When he'd climbed out, he said he wouldn't be long. I hoped that was true. Sitting in an abandoned parking lot in front of an abandoned building in the middle of nowhere was somewhat creepy. Okay, maybe it wasn't exactly the middle of nowhere, but it wasn't as if other buildings or people were around. Add to that the rain, the decaying body, and the fact that we were here to check out the place for a show about ghosts, and all the elements needed to send me into freakout mode seemed to be in play.

I tried to see if Tony was on his way back, but the windows had fogged up, which added to the feeling of isolation. When a shadow passed in front of the fogged-up window, and Tony didn't open the door and climb inside, I felt my heart accelerate. Not being able to see out the windows was very creepy, so when the rain on the roof seemed to have slowed to a sprinkle, I cracked open my window and hoped that would be enough to clear the windows a bit. Once that was done, I turned my attention to the warm breath on my neck.

"It's going to be okay," I assured Tilly as she sat in the back of the truck but leaned her head against the front seat, close to my ear. "I know you wanted to go with Tony and Mike, but it really is best that you stay here with me." She whined a bit, so I turned slightly to look her in the eye. "Are you worried about Daddy?"

She whined again.

"He's fine. He's with Uncle Mike, and he'll be right back."

I wasn't sure if Tilly understood me, but she seemed to be pacified by my explanation since she not only stopped whining but fully settled onto the backseat.

When Kiwi began to kick, I instinctively began to rub my stomach in a soothing, circular fashion. I knew that when I got stressed, it also stressed the baby, so I tried to relax. I'd heard music could soothe a restless baby, so sometimes I hummed to her since my singing voice wasn't the best. As I soothed myself and my baby, I let my mind wander. I'd likely have fallen asleep had I not heard a noise. I briefly held my breath before Tony opened the driver's side door and climbed in. He started the truck and turned on the defroster.

"So what did Mike say?" I asked.

"Not a lot. You know Mike, he's all business. He said that the coroner was on his way, and while he and Frank waited, they planned to look around to see if they could figure out what happened. Mike wanted me to leave the keys to the gate and theater with him, so I called Susan and filled her in on what was going on, and she said it was fine to pass the keys off to Mike." He leaned forward and adjusted the heater's vent to directly hit the window. "As for you and me, I think we're done here. Someone will need to call Jazzy to give her the bad news that the building will be inaccessible for at least a few days."

"I wonder if Mike will be done with his investigation by the time Tim and Tom plan to film next week."

Tony shrugged. "Maybe. I guess it depends on what, if anything, they find in the next day or two." Tony looked at his watch. "As for you, Tilly, and me, we can either continue to Kalispell to meet with the woman from the antique store, or I can call and reschedule, and we'll go home."

"Let's go ahead and meet with the woman. I feel fine, and it's not like there's anything more that we can do here."

Tony agreed with my plan, so he pulled away from the building and headed toward the driveway that led to the gate.

Chapter 4

Nancy Whelan was an intriguing woman. She was short, no taller than five feet at the very most, but she had a loud voice and a commanding presence that couldn't be ignored. The woman wore a colorful peasant-style dress, accentuating her bright red hair. Based on her general outward appearance, I'd say she was in her mid to late sixties, but she carried herself with an ease often found in women half her age.

"I must say that I've been tickled pink since I received the email confirming that my chest of drawers would be used on Tim and Tom's show." Her bright blue eyes lit up as she spoke. "I just love those men, and their show is so interesting. When I heard they were coming to Northern Montana again this year, I knew I had to write and tell them about my ghostly experiences."

I looked around the large room, which was so packed with antiques that I wasn't sure if Kiwi and I would even be able to make it through from the front to the back.

"You have a lot of very nice things for sale," Tony said, looking around the room. "But Tim and Tom have a lot of equipment and normally use a crew to film the segments they air, so I'm not sure this space will work."

"It won't?" The woman's smile faded.

"Maybe we can move the chest of drawers, or perhaps we can even find a way to clear out some space around the haunted item," I said. "Do you have the item here?"

She nodded, her head of red curls bouncing with the motion. Given her age and the brightness of her hair, I had to assume that hair dye had been used as an enhancement, but the color suited her. "I have the chest of drawers in the back. I realized I needed to remove it from the sales floor once Tim and Tom agreed to feature my shop in their show. We wouldn't want to sell it before they could film it now, would we?"

"It was a good idea to take it off the sales floor," Tony agreed. "Let's wander back and look at it. Maybe we can figure out a solution to the overcrowding problem."

I slowly followed Tony toward the rear of the building. It was a tight fit in places but manageable. The door at the back of the room led to a much less crowded storage, renovation, and office area. My attention was immediately drawn to the massive chest of drawers against the back wall. I don't know what I expected to see, but this piece of furniture, which took up nearly half the wall, certainly wasn't what I anticipated.

"This Gentleman's Chest is twelve feet wide and eight feet tall," Nancy began. "It was built in eighteen eighty-six by a Dutch craftsman named Aaron Benedict. Benedict arrived in the States as a young man and opened his own furniture store. He specialized in one-of-a-kind pieces and traveled from Boston to San Francisco when commissioned to build several pieces for a man named Walter Loganfield, who was a wealthy importer/exporter who was known for his love of fine furniture, fine wine, and beautiful women." She paused and took a deep breath. "I won't go into the details of the journey west or the challenges Benedict met as he tried to honor the contract he'd signed, but suffice it to say that at some point, it's said that the man lived to regret his decision to take on such a large project."

I was much more curious about the ghost than the history of the Gentleman's Chest, but I kept my mouth closed and just listened.

"Anyway," Nancy continued, "the wall unit Walter built consisted of imported wood that could only be found in the drier regions of Africa. As you can see, it's very unique, and it's said that Loganfield was the envy of all his friends until a rival shot him to death. After his death, his estate was passed down to his daughter, who closed off the master suite where her father died but continued to use the rest of the house. The daughter, an educated woman named Anya, told friends that while she didn't believe in ghosts, there had been some odd occurrences since her father's death that had her wondering. While Anya seldom spoke about the ghostly presence, she had documented her thoughts. According to journals written by Anya and discovered after she eventually passed, she concluded that her father's spirit had indeed survived his death."

"So Anya thought her father's ghost was haunting her?" I asked.

The woman confirmed that was the case. "Anya initially assumed that it was the house her father was haunting, so in her later years, she locked the place up and moved away. The house was unoccupied for a couple decades until Anya passed, and her son, Damian, inherited the place. Damian sold or donated most of the contents and then had the house torn down and the property auctioned off. Theoretically, bulldozing the house should have banished the ghost. But after the house was destroyed, strange things began happening to Damian, who eventually decided that the family ghost had followed him home. Someone figured out that the ghost was attached to the Gentleman's Chest, one of the items that Damian had kept, and the piece was put into storage at some point along the way. It was there until a few months ago when one of Damian's descendants put it up for auction, and I bought it."

"Did you know it was haunted?" I asked.

"I did."

"Then why did you buy it?"

The woman shrugged. "It sounded like a fun idea at the time."

I supposed buying a chest of drawers that you believed was haunted would add an element of excitement to your life. Given the size of the wall unit, I doubted the piece would have been easy to sell, even if it wasn't purported to be haunted. There was no way the unit was moved to its current location in one piece, so I had to assume the chest of drawers broke down into smaller, more manageable sections that could be transported and reassembled. Of course, if that were true, which section was the ghost attached to?

Tony and Nancy discussed leaving the piece where it currently stood and clearing out the area around it so that Tim and Tom had an unobstructed view for filming. Nancy thought that would work fine, and she promised to clear everything out within the boundaries Tony pointed out before Tim and Tom rolled into town this weekend.

After we left the antique shop, we headed to a nearby café for lunch. Kiwi and I were both starving, and the menu offered by this particular eatery looked both creative and delicious.

"So what time do we need to meet with Hannah about the haunting of the family estate by her dead sister, Beatrice?" I asked Tony after we'd ordered and our beverages had been delivered.

"I told her it would be mid-afternoon but wasn't specific beyond that. I thought I'd call her and confirm a time." Tony looked at his watch. "We are running behind schedule, but I think we can eat and still return to White Eagle by three-thirty."

"That works for me," I said. "Once we finish eating lunch, I want to call Bree to check in with her. I'm sure she's going stir-crazy by this point."

"I'm sure she is. We can stop by after we chat with Hannah if you'd like. Maybe that would take her mind off of things for a while."

"Maybe," I said. "I'll try to get a feel for Bree's mood when I call, and we can decide from there. Now that Mike has a new murder case to investigate, I suspect he might be late getting home this evening, so maybe we should bring Bree some food if we stop by."

"I am curious about the identity of the body we found," Tony said. "By this point, all that was left were bones, but I did notice an obvious hole in the skull of the skeleton, which seemed to indicate a shot to the head. I'm not sure why the victim or the shooter would be in the old theater, but I guess it might have been a meeting place."

"Or the victim was shot elsewhere and then taken to the theater after they were already dead," I suggested.

"I suppose that might be the case as well."

Lunch was delicious, but the conversation, which naturally centered around the skeleton Tilly had found that morning, did tend to suck the enjoyment out of the meal. Tony and I made a point of changing the subject during the drive back to White Eagle, so by the time we arrived at the Montrose Estate, we were back in a ghostly mindset rather than the cold-blooded killer mindset we found ourselves bogged down in during our meal.

Hannah seemed happy to see us and was more than a little thrilled to show us around the large estate that had been in her family for four generations. When Beatrice was alive, the sisters lived in the large house together, but Hannah found herself alone in the three-story structure after Beatrice died. As Hannah shared her grief and her loneliness, I became even more convinced than I had been that Hannah's ghost was actually just a figment of her imagination created to keep her company when no one else was around.

"Tess and I are here today to check the area where the filming is to take place for obstacles," Tony said. "The house and the estate are huge, so I don't think that not having enough room for the crew and all their equipment will be an issue, but I do wonder if there is a specific room or place on the grounds where Tim and Tom are more likely to run into Beatrice than other locations around the property."

"Either the suite that has belonged to Beatrice since she was a little girl or the stable where she liked to hang out. I still tend to find her presence in both locations since her death."

"Did Beatrice live here in this house her entire life?" Tony asked.

Hannah nodded. "Both Bea and I were born in this house, but I eventually married and moved out to live with my husband. Unfortunately, we were never able to have children, so I decided to move back home to live with Bea when my husband passed away. The two of us were very content with our arrangement until she got sick and eventually passed."

"Does anyone else live on the property?" Tony asked.

"Gus and Helen live in the caretaker's cottage on the south side of the lake. Gus takes care of the grounds and home maintenance, and Helen handles the cooking and oversees the maids who come in from town two times a week."

"So there's no other family?" Tony asked.

She hung her head. "No, our mother died when Bea and I were in our twenties, and then our father died just a year before I moved back home. I loved my parents, and while I miss them, there has never been a passing that left such a hole in my heart as Bea's passing." She looked directly at Tony. "I know it might sound odd to you that Bea would choose to stay behind in ghostly form, but I suspect she's worried about me. I want her to be able to move on. I want her to be happy and not unnaturally tied to this earthly plane, which led me to Tim and Tom. I'm hoping they can do what I've been unsuccessful doing."

"So you've tried to convince your sister to move on," I confirmed.

"I have, but Bea always was a stubborn one."

I really had no idea if Beatrice was haunting the house or not, but I could see that Hannah was lonely and unhappy, and helping her to move on to a meaningful life without her sister seemed to be the actual goal of any therapy session that might take place. I didn't have an immediate answer for Hannah's isolation, but I did feel for her. I seemed to have a lot of time on my hands since no one would let me do anything due to my pregnancy. Maybe I'd dig around a bit and see if I couldn't find a very earthly way to help Hannah let go and move on so that Beatrice could let go and move on.

Chapter 5

Once Tony and I had finished at the Montrose Estate, I called Bree. It was only five-thirty, and we technically had one more stop on our list, but it got dark early at this time of the year, so Tony and I decided it would be best to wait and visit the Stonewall Estate the following day. I asked Bree if Mike would be working late, and she confirmed that he had called and indicated that he might not be home quite as early as he originally planned. I asked her how she was feeling, and her answer was bored, so I offered to pick up some food and stop by. She was thrilled with the idea, so Tony called Shaggy to let him know that we'd be later than we'd originally planned and that it was okay to go ahead and leave after locking up.

Bree was in the mood for Chinese food, so we stopped by our favorite takeout place and ordered a selection of healthy options, including rice, veggies, spring rolls, and chicken and beef skewers. Mike had indicated he'd be late, but we figured he'd need to eat when he did get home, so we bought enough food for four.

"So you think the sister has created a ghost to keep her company," Bree confirmed after I'd brought her up to speed on the current situation unfolding at the Montrose Estate.

"I think it's a possibility. I do believe that Hannah believes she has been visited by the ghost of her dead sister. I admit that I don't know a lot about ghosts, so I'm certainly not qualified to say with any degree of certainty that the ghost is all in her head, but Beatrice died of natural causes after having lived a long life. Based on what Hannah shared, it didn't sound like her sister had any unfinished business." I picked up a veggie and chicken skewer and nibbled on a perfectly cooked piece of bell pepper. "In my opinion, Hannah is simply lonely and has created a ghost to fill the void."

"I guess I can understand that. It's sad to think of that poor woman living alone in that huge house. Maybe she should take on a roommate. It sounds as if she has a lot of extra bedrooms."

"There are unoccupied bedrooms," I agreed. "And a roommate isn't a bad idea. She said she didn't have family, but maybe a friend or someone who lives in the community might benefit from such an arrangement. Tony and I did what we needed to do to prepare things for Tim and Tom, so I'm not sure if we'll have a reason to stop at the Montrose Estate in the future, but if I am presented with the opportunity, I might chat with Hannah about the idea." I held up the container with the spring rolls. "Do you want another?"

Bree indicated that she did. It seemed we'd both concluded that healthy Chinese takeout, minus popular choices, which Tony had warned were heavy on salt, sugar, or MSG, wasn't exactly what we'd been craving.

Mike arrived home with his dog, Leonard, just as the three of us were finishing our meals. He headed toward the bedroom to change out of his uniform while Tony reheated the food. Once he returned and joined us at the kitchen table, Tony asked about the skeleton Tilly had found in the control room.

"I actually made quite a bit of progress today," Mike replied.

"Do you have an ID?" Tony asked.

"I'm still waiting for a DNA report, but based on what I do know, I feel fairly certain that our victim was Jake Black."

"Jake Black, the conspiracy theory guy?" I asked.

Mike confirmed that Jake Black, the conspiracy theorist, was the person he was referring to. Jake was a local man who worked at the lumber mill. He was an odd sort of fellow who was solitary and introverted, yet at the same time, oddly outspoken. The guy was best known for his controversial podcast, which seemed to be his platform to share his ideas with other local conspiracy theorists.

"Did you know that Jake was missing?" I asked.

"No," Mike replied. "At least not until today. Even though I'm still waiting for confirmation that the body in the morgue is indeed our favorite resident with a tall tale, I began to suspect that our murder victim was Jake after finding a silver medallion beneath his clothing. I remembered noticing the medallion around Jake's neck, so I called the lumber mill to see if he was still around. I spoke to his supervisor, who informed me that Jake hadn't been around for about eighteen months. I asked the man if he knew where Jake had gone and was told that Jake had been totally obsessed with one of his conspiracy theories and had missed work on multiple occasions, so when Jake failed to show up yet again, the supervisor left a message on his cell phone, telling him that he was fired and that his final check would be processed and mailed to him."

"So he never reported him as missing?" Bree asked.

"He did not," Mike confirmed.

"What about his landlord?" I asked.

"Jake lived in a little cabin on forest service land. He lived alone without direct neighbors, so no one missed him," Mike informed us. "Based on interviews I conducted today, there seemed to be some chatter in the conspiracy theory community about what might have happened to the guy when new podcasts weren't posted, but no one other than those in the community really paid much attention to the theories that began to circulate on the subject."

So this guy was shot and left in a locked room in a deserted building, and very few people even realized he was gone. I found that incredibly sad.

"Any idea who shot the guy or why he was shot in the first place?" Tony asked.

Mike answered. "Not yet, but I'm working on a few ideas. It occurred to me that Jake might have broken into the theater to research one of his ideas, and while he was there, he ran into someone who shot him and locked him in the control room. I realize the theory is quite broad, but it serves as a starting point. I have Frank and Gage looking into the subject of the podcasts he recorded and aired in the weeks before his death. Maybe he told his followers what he was working on and how he planned to research his latest topic."

"I suppose that if he did that, there might have been at least one listener who didn't want the guy poking around in what I can only assume had been a conspiracy theory based in fact," I said.

"That's my idea," Mike confirmed.

"There are groups on the web where like-minded individuals tend to congregate and share their theories," Tony said. "If you need help accessing these groups, just let me know. I'm happy to help in any way that I can."

"Thanks. I'll likely take you up on that. I guess at this point, I'm just hoping that if we can find out what

Jake was focused on in the weeks before he was shot in the head, then we can figure out what or whom we should be investigating."

While a conspiracy theory murder mystery seemed wildly intriguing to me, I could see that Bree was tired and probably was anxious to turn in, so I suggested to Tony that we head home. He agreed, so we said our goodbyes and headed toward the truck with Tilly trotting happily behind. Tilly loved spending time with Mike's dog, but Leonard was much younger than Tilly and tended to wear her out after a short time.

"Do you think Mike's idea that Jake was chasing a theory that ended up getting him killed is a good one?" I asked Tony as we headed up the mountain toward home.

"It makes sense to me. Most conspiracy theories contain a level of truth. If Jake stumbled onto a theory with an underlying truth that someone didn't want to be revealed, I can see how that might have led to murder."

"I didn't know the man well, or really at all, but I did know who he was, and I feel bad that things ended the way they did for him. The guy had some wild ideas, there's no denying that, but he seemed to be a good guy at heart."

Tony agreed that, from his perspective, the man appeared harmless.

"You know," Tony began, "Shaggy followed Jake's podcast. I wonder if he knows what Jake had been focused on during the days before he disappeared."

"I guess you can ask him. It isn't late. Call him when we get home."

As it turned out, according to Shaggy, during the last days before Jake went missing, he'd become completely obsessed with the death of some guy named Gavigan O'Leary.

Chapter 6

"So Shaggy didn't know that the man Jake was obsessed with and the ghost in the theater Tim and Tom planned to counsel were the same person?" Bree asked me the following morning. Tony had some things to share with Mike, so he'd dropped me off to visit with Bree while he headed to the police station. We had Tilly with us since we planned to head out to the Stonewall Estate once Tony returned, but she'd gone with Tony since Leonard was with Mike today.

"Apparently, he didn't put it together. Shaggy remembered Jake talking incessantly about some guy named Gavigan O'Leary to the point where Shaggy had stopped listening to the podcasts. He also said he'd been busy launching the new video game when the O'Leary podcasts were aired and only listened to bits and pieces of the program when he had time.

When Tim and Tom announced their intent to film one of the specials in the old theater a few weeks ago, he'd been mildly interested in the idea but hadn't paid much attention to the details of the project, including the ghost's name."

"So what does Shaggy think about the whole thing now that he knows that Jake was shot and his body was left in the theater?"

"He's all over it, of course. He said he planned to relisten to the podcasts, which I guess are still in the podcast archive for members to access."

Bree took a sip of her herbal tea. "It seems so odd to me that this guy just fell off the face of the earth eighteen months ago, and no one seemed to care enough to make an issue of it."

"I don't think that Jake was close to anyone. His podcast subscribers likely noticed that he wasn't around, but I guess none of them thought his disappearance warranted notification to the authorities."

"It is true that the conspiracy theory crowd doesn't seem to have much use for cops. Based on stories Mike has shared over the years, I guess I can see why those individuals weren't willing to get involved." Bree cringed and then adjusted her position on the sofa.

"Are you having contractions again?"

"I am," she admitted. "Mild ones. Not like the other day, but while they aren't as strong, they are a lot more regular."

"Does Mike know?"

"He does. He offered to stay home from work today, but the contractions aren't that bad, and I know he has a lot to accomplish before the baby comes. If the pain becomes intense, I'll call him. He said he'd keep his cell phone close by and turned on all day."

"If you can't get ahold of Mike and need something, call me," I said. "Tony and I are heading out to the Stonewall Estate to do the walk around that Tim and Tom asked for, but after that, I'm entirely free."

"I'll keep that in mind. I'm sure Mike will answer my call if things do get bad, but it is nice to know I have a backup waiting in the wings."

"You know I'm always here for you."

She smiled. "I know." Bree adjusted her position again but couldn't get comfortable so she got up and moved to the recliner. "So tell me about the Stonewall Estate. Who are Tim and Tom hoping to connect with?"

"Buford Stonewall," I answered. "I don't know the entire story, but apparently, Buford was born in a small town in Alabama around the turn of the century. He was an adventurous man who somehow stumbled onto a treasure map, which led him to a fortune in gold coins. It's said that after Buford's initial success, he became obsessed with treasure hunting and used his newfound wealth to make the trip west in search of another treasure he felt sure he was on track to find. The treasure he was initially going after was in Idaho up near the border, but he somehow became sidetracked in White Eagle on his way through Montana. In addition to the land that still belongs to the Stonewall family, he also purchased a lot of other land in the area. Eventually, he built the mansion that housed Stonewall descendants for several generations. After Samuel Stonewall, the last Stonewall directly descended from Buford, passed away without leaving an heir or a last will and testament, the question of who would inherit the Stonewall land and corresponding wealth became blurry. I guess the whole thing has been tied up in court ever since, which is why the house has remained empty."

"So Samuel never married or had children?" Bree asked.

"Not as far as I know. Tony told me Samuel was reclusive and lived alone on the property for years. I'm not sure what sort of life event turned him into the sort of person who never left his home, but based on what Tony told me, that seems to have been the case."

"That's really sad. I can understand why someone totally cut off from human contact might not bother with a will, but you would think someone would have sorted things out by this point. That place has been empty for years."

"I agree with you. I know that five or six cousins are fighting over the estate. One of the cousins has insisted from the beginning that Samuel had left a will, which, in his opinion, was being suppressed, but that assertion never seemed to go anywhere. In fact, the cousin who asserted that the will existed also suggested that the document had been found and destroyed by one of the other cousins who came out on the short end. I think there may also be a non-family member who has staked a claim. I don't know the details, but Tony said there has been an effort to locate a will. So far, no one seems to have had any success. There are those who feel certain that if Samuel had drawn one up, he would have made sure it got into the right hands, while others seem to think the document might be hidden on the estate."

"Why would Samuel make out a will and then hide it rather than filing it with his attorney?" Bree asked.

"That's a good question. The whole thing makes no sense. I don't know why the cousins don't join forces and figure out how to settle the estate. If they could agree on something, at the very least, they'd each get a slice of the pie. The way it is now, no one has access to the property or the cash."

"Maybe there's more to it," Bree said. "Maybe something is going on beyond a missing will. Something worth a lot more money than the house and land. Something the cousins know about but don't want to admit."

"Like what?"

"Buford was a treasure hunter, so maybe there's another treasure in play. One that Buford talked about with his family but never found."

"Maybe," I agreed. "But Buford lived in that house more than a hundred years ago. If there was a treasure and he talked about it to his family, it seems as if a child or grandchild would have found it long before this."

"I suppose you make a good point. It still might be true that old Buford hid something the cousins are trying to find."

"If Tim and Tom are successful in their attempt to connect with Buford, perhaps he can tell them where to find whatever it is that everyone is looking for."

Tony and Tilly returned while Bree and I discussed the idea of a treasure. He was intrigued by the idea, but to this point, no one had mentioned a treasure, and as I had already pointed out, Buford died a long time ago, and many people had lived on the estate since that time. I ensured that Bree was settled and had her cell phone close at hand, and then I headed to the truck with my husband and dog.

"Does it seem odd to you that the estate would be tied up in one lawsuit after another for what has, by this point, amounted to years?" I asked Tony as we drove out of town toward the property.

"It does, but I doubt this is the first time something like this has happened. A lot of money is involved, and without a will, it's likely difficult to determine who deserves what."

"Bree and I were just saying that it was extremely odd that Samuel didn't leave a last will and testament with his attorney. The guy was born into a wealthy family. I'm sure he understood how important such things are when you have wealth to leave to whoever should receive it."

Tony frowned. "Yeah, the story of the hidden will doesn't really work for me. Of course, the idea that the man didn't have a will doesn't work either. I'm personally on board with the idea of a document that has been suppressed for some reason."

"If that's true, the attorney has to be in on it."

"I guess he might be."

"Who has been managing the estate since Samuel died?" I asked.

"His attorney."

"So maybe it's true that a will hasn't been found because of the attorney. He's being paid to manage the property. If the estate had been settled early on, he would have lost decades of income."

Tony turned and glanced in my direction. "As unlikely as that sounds, it does seem to be the best explanation currently on the table."

Pulling off the highway and onto a frontage road, Tony slowed as he neared the private drive that led out to the estate. At one point, the property had been professionally landscaped with sweeping lawns and groomed flowerbeds, but all that had survived were weeds entangled amongst the shrubs that had been hearty enough to make it on their own.

The mansion was in decent shape, although it would have benefited from a coat of paint. The porch railing was wobbly, but other than that, the mansion's exterior seemed to have held up okay. Tony used the key Jazzy had sent him to open the front door. The windows had all been boarded up, giving the interior a cave-like feel despite the sunny day. The air temperature within the structure was near freezing, which had me wishing I'd worn my heavy jacket rather than the long-sleeved t-shirt I'd chosen when I'd realized we were in for a warm, sunny day.

"Given the fact that it has stood empty for a good number of years, I was expecting the place to be trashed, but except for the fact that it's freezing, it's not too bad in here." I ran a finger over a table. "It's not even all that dusty."

"I think the property management company sends a crew out to clean and take care of maintenance issues a few times a year."

"The garden is a mess," I pointed out.

Tony shrugged. "I guess the property manager isn't worried about the garden so much as protecting the house's integrity."

"There appears to be ample space for Tim and Tom to set up. Does the electrical work?"

Tony walked down a hallway to a doorway about two-thirds of the way down. He opened the door to reveal an electrical panel. When Tony flipped the switch, the lights and the heater clicked on. "It does," he confirmed.

"I wonder why they don't just leave the heat on so that it doesn't get so cold in here," I commented as I rubbed my arms.

Tony walked further down the hallway and looked at the thermostat. "It's still a good ten degrees above freezing, and I imagine that leaving the heater on over the summer wouldn't have been necessary. I suspect they activate the power to prevent the pipes from freezing when the severe cold weather arrives." Tony pulled his cell phone out. "I'm going to walk around and take the photos Jazzy wanted. Do you and Tilly want to walk with me, or would you prefer to wait outside where it's warmer?"

"I think we'll wait outside," I said.

Stepping into the warm sunshine felt wonderful after spending even a short amount of time in the cold, dark interior of the home. I wondered if Tim and Tom planned to take the plywood off the windows for the taping. Since the taping was to occur after sunset, I figured that it was unlikely that they'd bother. I doubted they'd even use the overhead lights once they got set up since specialized mood lighting would provide a much better effect for a ghost hunt.

"Let's go and look at the barn, Tilly." I figured Tony would be inside at least thirty minutes, and the red barn with a black door and black shutters in the distance seemed welcoming and picturesque against the deep blue sky.

Unfortunately, the barn was locked, preventing us from entering, but the view from the rear of the large building was even more fantastic than the view from the front, so I still considered the walk worth the effort. As I stood looking out over rolling hills that seemed to go on forever, I wondered once again why Samuel hadn't made more of an effort to resolve matters for the benefit of his family. The man had to have known that the family would do as they seemed to have done and spend the next decade embroiled in disputes over it without a document clearly spelling out who inherited the estate.

"Can I help you with something?"

I turned around and found a tall man wearing black jeans, a red and white plaid shirt, and a black cowboy hat standing behind me. "You startled me. I didn't hear you arrive."

The man just continued to stare at me.

"My name is Tess Marconi." I put a hand on Tilly's head to let her know things were okay since she'd begun to growl. "This is Tilly. We're here with my husband, Tony Marconi. He's inside taking photos for Tim and Tom."

"The *Ghost Therapy* guys?"

I nodded, and the man frowned.

"He has a key and permission to be here," I said. "I'm sure you saw our truck parked in front of the house."

"I did see the truck. I knew Marblehead, in his infinite wisdom, decided to allow a whole passel of folks to spend the night out here on the property, but I didn't realize anyone would be around until Saturday."

"Marblehead?"

"Art Morehead, the attorney overseeing the management of the place while ownership issues are dealt with."

"Oh, I see." I guess Marblehead was a natural progression from Morehead if the man in front of me didn't like the guy. "And who are you?"

"Lawrence Hightower. I'm one of the six cousins still in contention for a piece of this place. I live closer than the others, so I offered to come by and occasionally look in on things. I knew the *Ghost Therapy* folks planned to spend time here next week, so I figured I'd come by to confirm that the place survived that big storm we had a few weeks ago."

The area had recently suffered one of the worst summer storms I could remember. Not only had there been severe flooding in the low-lying areas, but there had also been damaging winds. Luckily, there hadn't been any damage to the town itself, but there had been reports of damage to a few outlying areas.

"I guess I'll head inside and chat with your husband." He looked toward the far eastern side of the barn. "There's a tree down over there, so it's best you just backtrack and head back the way you came."

"I'll do that."

The man tipped his hat and walked away. Lawrence had been cordial enough, and while it sounded like he had every reason to be here, there was something about the way he kept nervously glancing around that made me wonder if the man hadn't been here for a reason other than what he'd offered.

I didn't suppose that Lawrence's real agenda, should he have one, was any of my business or concern, so I looked at the fabulous view a final time before I headed back around the barn from the same direction I'd come as Lawrence had suggested. When I arrived at the truck, Tony emerged from the doorway that led to the mansion's interior.

"Did you hook up with Lawrence?" I asked.

"I did," Tony confirmed. "I guess he's here to check on a few things before the *Ghost Therapy* crew arrives next week, so I took my photos and got out of the way. You all set?"

"Tilly and I are ready to go." I looked up at the house one last time and noticed for the first time that a window at the very top of the house, which I imagined must be the attic, hadn't been covered with wood the way other windows had been. "Did you see that?"

"See what?" Tony asked as he turned his key in the ignition.

"The window at the top of the house. I swear I saw someone looking out."

"Maybe it was Lawrence."

"It wasn't Lawrence. I think it was a woman. Did you notice anyone other than Lawrence inside when you were taking your photos?"

"No."

"Did you go in the room at the top of the house?"

He looked up at the window. "No. I didn't notice an access to a room above the second story."

"If the room is an attic, it may be accessed by a pull-down ladder or that sort of thing."

"I suppose that could be true." Tony looked up at the room again. "I don't think taking photos of that space will be necessary. If Tim and Tom plan to film the episode in an area large enough for spectator participation, they aren't going to mess around with a room that needs to be accessed via a pull-down ladder."

Even though I suspected that was true, I was still interested in learning about the woman I'd seen in the window. I was about to ask Tony if he'd try to find the entrance and take a few photos anyway when another truck pulled in, and a cowboy equally as tall as Lawrence emerged. As Lawrence had with me, the man who emerged from the black truck asked about our presence on private property, and as I had done with Lawrence, Tony explained the reason for our business. The man didn't look any happier about us being there than Lawrence had, so when he suggested that we ought to get along now that we'd done what we came for, Tony agreed.

"It's a shame we never got to check out the attic," I said as Tony merged onto the highway.

"The guy in the black truck seemed pretty upset that we were there. I figured it was best not to push it."

"Lawrence told me he was one of the cousins currently fighting for a piece of the property. Do you think the man in the black truck was another cousin?"

"I'm not sure. Maybe. I think I'll pull over to call Jazzy to fill her in on what's going on at the estate. She's the one who made all the arrangements for Tim and Tom's visit, so she would know who to contact if she felt it was important to notify someone about the men currently on the property."

Tony stepped out of the vehicle to make his call. I couldn't hear everything they said, but it sounded as if Jazzy planned to follow up with the attorney in charge of the estate. When Tony got back into the truck, he had a frown on his face.

"Is something wrong?" I asked.

"While Jazzy and I were talking, she informed me that Tim and Tom have decided to adjust their schedule to allow for a multi-part session at the theater."

"Adjust their schedule?" I asked. "Adjust their schedule, how?"

"I guess they are a lot more interested in the murdered usher and the much more recent murder of the conspiracy theorist investigating the murder of the usher than they are in furniture ghosts or dead sisters. They plan to reduce the segments involving the haunted chest of drawers and the ghost at the Montrose Estate to a brief clip that will provide a history of the alleged ghosts, which they will film on Sunday and Monday. They will begin filming at the theater on Tuesday or as soon as the police allow them access."

"Do you need to notify Nancy and Hannah about the change to their filming schedule?"

"No, Jazzy is taking care of that, so all she needs us to do is to let her know if we learn anything about

76

Jake's death and to be available for Tim and Tom once they arrive in town should they need help either at the theater or the Stonewall Estate."

I was actually happy to hear that our workload wouldn't increase since, in addition to our roles of overseers for the filming of *Ghost Therapy*, Tony and I were also responsible for making sure that the kiddie carnival, craft fair, Halloween parade, and the chili cookoff all went off without a hitch.

Chapter 7

Shortly after we returned home, Mike called and spoke to Tony about the murder case he was working on. He admitted that he could use Tony's help with the conspiracy theorist who liked to spend time on the dark web, so Tony invited him over so they could brainstorm. Bree was feeling okay but going a bit stir-crazy, so we invited them to come for dinner.

"It's so peaceful out here," Bree said as she and I sat on the deck in comfy loungers, sipping on the virgin mojitos Tony had made for us. "If you sit quietly, all you can hear are the birds."

"I truly love it out here, which is causing me to be conflicted about moving into town. I know that once Nella is old enough for school, moving makes the most sense, but I really will miss this."

"Nella?" Bree asked. "Have you decided on a name?"

I paused. "Sort of. Tony would like to name our daughter after Nona, and, in concept, I'm all for that. Nona's birth name was Antonella, which is a beautiful name but quite the mouthful for a child. Tony and I discussed the idea of using a nickname for everyday use, and we both agreed that of all the nicknames derived from Antonella, either Toni or Ella are the best. But as you know, we already have a Tony and an Ella in the family."

"So you decided on Nella?"

I shook my head. "No. I've been trying out names, but none have stuck. Nella is just my latest attempt to find something that feels right."

"What about Tina or Anna."

I screwed up my face. "Both are fine names, but I'm not sure either is quite right."

"Have you settled on a middle name?"

"We kicked around the idea of Theresa after Mom and me, but I won't go so far as to say we settled on it for certain."

"What about Tori for a nickname. Or even Thea. I don't suppose either is a direct nickname for Theresa, but they seem close enough to work."

"You know, I have been seriously considering the idea of a "T" name. We have Tess, Tony, Tilly, Titan, Tang, and Tinder. Kody is the odd man out, and I've always wished I'd given him a "T" name when he came to live with us, even though the breeder had already named him Kody when he joined the family. It's too late to change it now, but staying with a "T" name does feel right." I paused for just a moment and then tried out Bree's suggestion. "Tess, Tony, and Thea. I don't hate it, but I like Theo a little more than I like Thea."

"What about Thomas for a middle name rather than Theresa? I know our son will be Michael Tucker Thomas, but I don't think using Thomas as a middle name for your daughter will be confusing."

"Antonella Thomas Marconi," I said aloud. I smiled. "I like it. Using Thomas as the middle name not only links my daughter to me but to my entire family." I bit down on my lower lip. "I like the idea, but I'm not sure that helps me with a nickname."

"You like Toni and Theo. Both are traditionally boy names, but it seems that these days anything goes. How about Tommi, which would be short for Thomas. Tommi spelled with an 'i,' so it has a feminine touch."

"Tommi," I said aloud. I allowed the name to roll around in my mind a bit. "I like Tommi. I like Theo as well. Thanks for the suggestion. I'll talk to Tony about it."

"Happy to help."

The sun had just set when Mike joined us on the patio. Tony had headed to the kitchen to put the lasagna he made earlier into the oven.

"So, how'd it go?" Bree asked.

"I think we made a lot of progress. It appears like Jake had put a lot of time into trying to solve the Gavigan O'Leary murder. He might have been an odd guy on the surface who tended to go off on one rant or another, but the notes he left behind indicate that he was also intuitive and intelligent. In fact, I actually think that with the notes he left, Tony and I might be able to solve the case after all these years."

"Be careful," Bree said. She rubbed her stomach. "Michael is going to need his father, and it looks as if whatever it was that O'Leary managed to uncover about the death of the movie theater usher is likely what led to his death."

Mike smiled at his wife. "I'll be careful. At this point, Tony and I are only digging up podcasts, blogs, emails, and chat room posts left behind by Black. We plan to return to the movie theater tomorrow to take another look around, but I'll bring Frank and Gage with me, and we'll be fully armed."

"So, who's hungry?" I asked since Bree was scowling at Mike at this point. Mike was a cop, and his job occasionally put him in dangerous situations, and Bree knew that. I supposed the fact that she was due to deliver the couple's second child any day now that had her on edge. I guessed I could understand that. I was usually pretty laid back about the dangerous aspects of the various investigations that Mike, Tony, and I tended to stumble into, and even I had been feeling more and more vulnerable since I found out about Kiwi and realized that I was now responsible for her life as well as my own.

"I, for one, am starving," Bree said. "Not that I can eat all that much. My doctor wants me to stick to small meals until Michael is born, but even a few bites of Tony's lasagna will be heavenly."

Everyone agreed not to discuss the murder case during the meal, but as soon as we'd finished and everyone had retired to the living room, I jumped in and demanded an update.

Mike took the lead. "I'm not sure how Jake latched onto his theories. There are several. The theory that seemed to be most recent was the idea that a local politician stabbed O'Leary to death rather than a deranged horror movie fan as the police suspected at the time."

"Politician?" I asked.

Mike shrugged.

"I'm not sure I ever heard the original story, so someone needs to catch me up," Bree said.

"Gavigan O'Leary was an usher who worked in the old movie theater on the highway before the new theater in town was built," Mike said. "He was stabbed to death, and his body was found behind the screen in nineteen ninety-five. The police investigated, but there didn't seem to be a clear suspect or motive, so they eventually decided that O'Leary was stabbed by a deranged moviegoer after viewing a particularly gruesome slasher movie where the killer stabbed his victims twelve times in a pattern very similar to the one used to stab O'Leary to death."

"But this conspiracy theory guy thought otherwise?" Bree asked.

Mike nodded. "Jake Black seemed to think that O'Leary had seen something he shouldn't have. It was his belief that the individual who stabbed O'Leary replicated the stabbing scene in the movie to throw the police off their scent. If Jake was correct and the twelve stab wounds were simply a decoy to hide the real motive behind the killing, then the killer's plan seems to have worked."

"Okay," Bree said. "I think I'm all caught up. Who exactly did Jake think killed O'Leary?"

Tony answered this time. "He didn't know, but he suspected that the killing had to do with the political upheaval that was going on in the area at the time."

"Political upheaval?" Bree asked.

Tony continued. "A new mayor had been elected the previous year, and while the man initially ran on a platform of a governing body responsive to the needs of the people, what really happened was that the governing body the new mayor put into place seemed to support the ideas of a handful of wealthy and powerful men rather than the general population."

"Do we know who these rich and powerful men were?" Bree inquired.

"Richmond Stonewall, for one."

"Richmond Stonewall, as in the Stonewall Estate?" I asked.

Tony nodded. "Richmond Stonewall was Samuel Stonewall's father. He died in nineteen ninety-eight, and Samuel inherited the house and the land. Samuel had been reclusive from a young age and already had established himself as a bit of a hermit by the time his father passed. Samuel never married or had children, so he didn't leave a direct heir to inherit his wealth. As we know, Samuel's death is what set up the battle currently being carried out by cousins, who, based on what I understand, are linked to the Stonewalls through Samuel's mother, who had three siblings."

"And the interesting part," Mike added, "is that the old theater, where both Jake and O'Leary appeared to have been murdered, was originally built by Douglas Stonewall, who passed the building down to Richmond, who passed it down to Samuel."

"The probate that has left the old theater sitting all this time is the same probate that has left the Stonewall Estate sitting all this time," I said.

Mike confirmed that fact.

"Okay," I said, hoping to return to the original discussion. "So Jake believed that there was a group of powerful men in the area who seemed to have their own agenda when Gavigan O'Leary was stabbed to death in nineteen ninety-five. They used their wealth and influence to put individuals they controlled into office, and Black suspected it was one or more of these men who killed O'Leary after O'Leary learned something he shouldn't have."

"That was Black's theory," Mike said. "And I'm not just talking at a local level. In addition to the mayor, Black seemed to think that this group also controlled a couple of senators and representatives on both the state and national level."

Tony jumped back in. "Let's keep in mind that while rich and powerful men often tend to be politically connected, at this point, we have zero proof of wrongdoing of any of the men on the list. All we have are the ramblings of a man who had been convinced he'd stumbled onto a huge conspiracy."

"But it is at least possible that Black was onto something," Bree said.

"It is at least possible," Mike agreed. "Black speculated Gavigan O'Leary must have witnessed or overheard something he wasn't supposed to. Something that would have incriminated one or more of the men who had developed a brotherhood to benefit their agendas. It was Black's opinion that whatever O'Leary had overseen or overheard, he'd overseen or overheard it at the theater. He was also convinced that proof of whatever it was that O'Leary was killed for still existed, and the place to find it was within the walls of the old building."

"So O'Leary was cleaning up after the slasher movie ended, and someone used a knife to stab him to death," I said. "Then more than a quarter century after O'Leary was stabbed to death, Jake Black decides to check out the scene of the crime and is shot to death." I glanced at Tony. "Do you know what Jake was looking for on the night he died?"

"Not yet, but Mike and I plan to continue to dig. I feel as if we've only scratched the surface of the case

Jake was building in the short time we had to dig into things before we stopped our search and came up to have dinner."

"I have a question." Bree raised her hand as if she was in a classroom.

"What's your question?" Mike asked.

"If Gavigan O'Leary was killed because of something he saw or overheard, and if it was Jake's theory that he was exposed to this information while working at the theater, that means the men involved in this political scandal, if that is even what was going on, met in the theater to either do something or discuss something. Why? Of all the places available to meet, why there?"

"That's actually a great question," Mike said.

That had Bree smiling with pride.

"And one we can't currently answer," Tony added.

"Who was the mayor back then?" I asked. I was around then, but I was just a kid and much too young to pay attention to politics.

"The mayor elected in nineteen ninety-four was a man named Homer Hamburg," Mike said. "He wasn't a likely pick since he had no experience in politics or city government, but he ran a clever campaign that got him elected."

"And how long did he serve as mayor?" I asked.

"Less than a year. Hamburg was elected in November of nineteen ninety-four, and he was killed in an auto accident in September of nineteen ninety-five, just four months after Gavigan O'Leary was found stabbed to death in the theater."

"So maybe his powerful buddies decided he knew too much," Bree said.

"Perhaps," Tony agreed.

"Other than Richmond Stonewall, do we know who else was part of this group?" I asked Tony.

"Jake left a list, but let's not forget that none of this has been proven."

"Are there any men with the last name of Weston or Wade on the list?" I asked.

Tony confirmed that to be the case. I wasn't surprised. If a group of rich and powerful men had joined forces to accomplish an undisclosed objective, you could bet the Westons and the Wades would be intricately involved.

Chapter 8

I decided to discuss the subject of a name for Kiwi over breakfast. I realized that Tony and I had dedicated considerable time discussing the subject, but the correct name was crucial, and I was determined to make the right choice. So far, I had rejected some names, while others were still on the "maybe" list, but I wasn't sure I'd settled on the perfect name.

I decided to begin by suggesting the idea of a "T" name. We'd discussed this before but hadn't decided whether or not to go this route. "I was talking to Bree yesterday, and I realized I really want our daughter to have a "T" name, or at least a "T" nickname. I wasn't sure if we should go for another "T" name to go with Tess, Tony, Tilly, Titan, Tang, and Tinder, but I feel so bad that we didn't give Kody a "T" name when he came to live with us, and I know I'll regret not going there for my child."

"A "T" name is fine with me," Tony said as Tilly looked up and thumped her tail.

"I do like the idea of Antonella after Nona as her official first name, and while I originally considered Theresa for a middle name, Bree suggested Thomas for a middle name, and I like that as well."

"I'm fine with either," Tony said.

"As we discussed, the obvious nicknames of Toni and Ella are taken, but what about either Tommi or Theo?"

Tony didn't answer right away. I could see that he was thinking it over.

"Bree suggested Tommi spelled with an 'i' for a girl, which would play nicely off our middle name of Thomas. Theo initially came about as a nickname for a boy, but then I realized I liked it for a girl as well." I folded my napkin in my lap. I wasn't sure why this conversation was making me nervous, but it was. It would have been better if Tony had jumped up and professed his love of one name or the other, but his silence was unnerving.

Eventually, Tony began to speak. "I know that our daughter is going to grow up to be her own person, and any images I may have in my mind are nothing more than speculation at this point, but I have to admit that I've been picturing our daughter as a tomboy like her mama. I'm not sure why. I will be just as happy if our daughter decides on ballet over baseball since my biggest hope for her is that she live her best life and be her own person, but every time I think of her I see a dark-haired little spitfire wearing a baseball cap over pigtails while she strikes out the boys on the opposing team."

I smiled. "That's how I picture our daughter, too, probably because I was the tomboy who had no time for dolls and preferred baseball over dance or gymnastics any day of the week." I looked at Tony. "So, about a name? Does the image in your mind look and feel like a Theo or Tommi to you?"

He nodded. "I like them both. I also like Teddi if we're strictly looking at "T" names and aren't trying to directly link it as a nickname for Thomas. Let's noodle on the idea for a few days and see if one name settles to the top."

"That idea is fine with me." I spread some of Tony's homemade jam on my biscuit. "So, what exactly is the plan for today?"

"Mike and I are going to the theater to look around again. We both want you and Bree to sit this one out, so you can wait here for me, or I can drop you by Bree's if she feels up for a visit."

"I'll just wait here. I'm feeling tired after the last couple of days. I think that I'll take it easy today."

"That sounds like a perfect idea."

After Tony left, I headed out onto the deck with my animals and my gynecologist-approved herbal tea. It was a beautiful morning, but the forecast called for rain later in the day. It had been a dry summer, and rain would be welcome, but I was determined to enjoy the sunshine as long as I had it. I was contemplating the idea of calling my mother to check in since I hadn't seen her in over a week when my dad pulled up in the new Jeep he'd bought. I waved to him from the patio, and he headed toward me. It was odd seeing Dad now that his transformation from secret agent man to regular guy was complete. I knew the man who walked toward me was my dad, but it's unlikely that I would have recognized him if I hadn't been around for all the phases of his transformation. He'd gained some weight and had plastic surgery to fill out his cheeks and reshape his nose. He wore colored contacts when he was out in public and had accentuated the gray in his hair so that the deep brown hair he'd always had was nothing more than a memory.

"Tess," he said with a lazy drawl that was nothing like the deep, commanding voice I was used to.

"Good morning, Dad. Every time I see you, you look less and less like the dad I've always known."

"That's the idea."

I supposed it was. The only way a man with a past such as the past my father had amassed could ever be free was to become an entirely different person.

"It looks as if the scars from your surgery are healing nicely. I can barely even tell you had surgery."

"I'm hoping I will be able to integrate into White Eagle as its newest resident by Thanksgiving."

I smiled. "Are you planning a launch party?"

He laughed. "Not exactly, but once I feel ready to officially join the community, I think I'll ask your mother to introduce me around town as an old friend who recently moved to White Eagle. If I can fool folks I used to know fairly well, I'll be confident that I can fool anyone who might still have reason to do me harm."

"Have you settled on a new name?"

Dad handed me a very authentic-looking driver's license.

"Hank Hannigan," I read aloud.

"Do I look like a Hank?"

I grinned. "Between the weight you've gained, your round cheeks, the bleach you've applied to your brown hair to turn it white, and the scraggly beard you've been working on, you sort of look like Santa Claus."

He frowned. "Santa Claus?"

"I'm just kidding. You look great, and most importantly, you look nothing like Grant Thomas. I think Hank is a fine name. Easy to remember, and it has a rugged feel to it." I returned his new driver's license. "So, do you have a new birth certificate and passport to go with your new driver's license?"

"I do. I have a new history as well. Should anyone decide to go to the trouble of looking up Hank Hannigan from Cottonwood Falls, Kansas, they'll find everything from a write-up in the newspaper featuring my Little League stats the year my team went to the state playoffs to my high school transcripts, which to keep it believable, are less than stellar."

"That's really amazing."

He shrugged. "Not really. Fake histories to support new identities are created more often than one might think."

There were times such as now when I felt sure I'd fallen asleep one night only to awaken in the Twilight Zone.

"Can I get you some coffee?" I asked.

"I'm fine. I can't stay long. I just wanted to stop by and see how you were doing."

"I'm fine." I put a hand on my stomach. "Kiwi is active today, which can become tiring after a while, but I feel pretty good compared to how I felt during the first few months."

"Still calling her Kiwi? I thought you might have settled on a name by now."

"Actually, we're getting close. Tony wants to name the baby Antonella after Nona, and I've decided on Thomas for a middle name in honor of my entire family."

"I like both names."

"So do I. It's just that Antonella Thomas Marconi seems like a big name for such a tiny baby. The whole name thing only works for me if we can settle on a cute and easy nickname."

"Do you have one in mind?" Dad asked.

"Actually, I've been kicking around the idea of calling her Tommi spelled with an 'i.'"

Dad's eyes grew wide. "Really?"

"Is there a problem with that?"

"No. The opposite, actually. Your grandmother was named Thomasina, and I chose the surname Thomas to honor her when I decided to marry and have children. She died when I was fairly young, but I remember her as being a real spitfire. Ninety-eight pounds of sheer energy. Everyone called her Tommy, spelled with a 'y.'"

"Tommy. Your mother was nicknamed Tommy?"

He nodded.

"That's the first time you've ever talked about your real family. My real family."

"And doing so was probably a bad idea, so how about we keep this between us. Even if someone knew my mother's birth name was Thomasina, there's no way they could unravel my new identity, but why risk it."

"I want to share this with Tony since it will help him understand why I am indisputably giving our baby the nickname Tommi rather than one of the other options, but I won't tell anyone else. I do think you should tell Mike."

He shrugged. "Maybe I will. He turned out okay. Seems to be the sort who can keep a secret."

I just rolled my eyes. Turned out okay? Saying something like that was so like Dad. Talk about suppressing any real emotions. "And my grandfather. Your father. Are you willing to share his name?"

"I don't know it. Never did. Mom told me that my father died before I was born. She looked so sad when she shared this with me that I never brought it up again."

"And then she died."

"And then she died."

"And you? What happened to you?"

Dad stood up. "That my, Tessie, is a story for another day." He turned around and looked back toward the house. "I take it Tony isn't around."

"He's in town with Mike. He should be back in a couple hours. Did you need him for something?"

"I wanted him to test out my new identity. If Tony can't detect a glitch or a flaw using his high-tech computer, then it's reasonable to assume that I'm safe from anyone else discovering that Hank Hannigan was, in fact, born yesterday."

"I'm sure Tony will be happy to help you. You're welcome to wait for him or return if you can't stay now."

"I'll wait. And maybe I will have that cup of coffee."

That honestly shocked me. Dad has always been the sort to pop in and pop out, never staying in any one place for long. Maybe he really was planning to stay around this time.

"So, is Tony helping Mike with a case?" Dad asked after we'd moved indoors, and I'd made coffee.

"He is." I went on to explain about Tim and Tom and their ghost therapy show, their intention to counsel the ghost of Gavigan O'Leary, who they felt sure was still haunting the old theater, and the discovery of the body of a conspiracy theorist, Jake Black, while Tony and I were scoping the place out ahead of the arrival of the *Ghost Therapy* cast and crew.

"I remember when the usher was found stabbed to death," Dad said.

It was true that Dad had been living in White Eagle during the nineties. He didn't fake his death until I was fourteen. "Do you remember anything specific about the incident? Something that might help Mike and Tony figure out what happened to Gavigan O'Leary and Jake Black."

"The theory at the time was that O'Leary was killed by a moviegoer who had become overly stimulated by the violence on the screen and had acted on his violent tendencies. I never really bought that. I guess there might have been someone viewing the movie who was also hopped up on drugs, which led to the enhancement of his emotions as well as the inhibition of his impulses. But I always thought it was more likely that a motivated individual with a singular purpose actually did away with the guy."

"Any idea who?" I asked.

"Not really. I had my own assignments to worry about, so I didn't involve myself in any way. The cops felt they had their explanation, and while I never agreed with it, I didn't do anything to try to offer another option."

"Jake thought that O'Leary was murdered because of something he knew. Something he likely overheard or even witnessed while doing his job."

"I suppose that might have been the case. Makes more sense than a man driven to commit a horrible murder after viewing a slasher movie."

"It does," I agreed. "While Jake's theories don't constitute facts, he did provide a list of wealthy and influential men who seemed to run things at the time. Jake was certain one or more of these men were behind the murder."

"Jake was focused on the Westons and the Wades."

"Amongst other people," I confirmed. "Mike mentioned a broad list that included the obvious suspects but also included men such as Richmond Stonewall."

I watched Dad's eyes as he considered this piece of information.

"Rich was a hard man. He had very definite views, and, in his mind, anyone who might have a way of looking at things that differed from his way of thinking was nothing more than pond scum."

"Sounds like a real peach. No wonder Samuel was such a recluse. He probably started hiding from his dad and never learned to integrate into society."

"That may well have been the case."

"Do you think Richmond Stonewall could have killed Gavigan O'Leary?"

Dad took a moment or two to think it over. "Could he have; yes. Did he; not necessarily. I understand where this conspiracy theory guy may have been coming from, but for as long as there have been communities of people, there have been those in charge and those who follow. The fact that White Eagle had, and still has, its own group of wealthy and influential men who tend to shape and steer local policies to benefit their own agendas is neither a novel nor an unexpected concept. But to carry out such a brutal murder when a single gunshot to the head would suffice suggests something more was going on. If one or more of these men does turn out to be the killer, I'll be surprised."

"Jake was killed with a single gunshot to the head."

"Then a killer simply wanting to shut the man up makes sense."

Dad had made some good points.

"So if you don't think the individual who stabbed Gavigan O'Leary was a moviegoer gone crazy or a member of this elite group who apparently still runs things, then who do you think did it?"

He shrugged. "Twelve stab wounds to the torso seems like a crime of passion, so I'd look for a jealous husband of a woman O'Leary may have been sleeping with, an individual who felt they had been damaged financially due to the actions of the victim, or even a rival for the affection of the man's one true love, assuming, of course, that he had one."

"What if you and Jake are both right. What if O'Leary's death was a crime of passion, but what if the individual who passionately killed the man also happened to be a member of this elite behind-the-scenes governing group."

"I suppose it's possible O'Leary wronged one of the men on the conspiracy theory guy's list, which would account both for the number of stab wounds to the body and the link to local politics that I assume this man must have claimed to have found."

"Mike wasn't sure what O'Leary had found that caused him to suspect someone from this group, but I'm sure he'll figure it out with Tony's help."

"I'm sure he will."

Tony came home sooner than I'd anticipated. After a brief kiss hello and the assurance that he'd fill me in on his morning with Mike later, he disappeared to the cleanroom in the basement with my dad, so I headed upstairs to rock in the chair I'd bought for the nursery and dream about the daughter I was becoming more and more anxious to meet."

Chapter 9

Dad and Tony were in the basement for about two hours. When they finally emerged, Dad kissed me on the cheek and left, and Tony escorted me into the kitchen with the idea of scrounging up something for lunch.

"How did your 'crack the ID' session with Dad go?" I asked Tony after I slid onto one of the barstools at the counter.

"So far, so good. I'm treating this like any other hacking case where I'm diligently trying to find a fracture in the security to allow me in. So far, I haven't found one, but I plan to keep trying."

"If a weakness or omission does exist, I guess it would be best for you to find it rather than someone else."

"Exactly. How about a grilled cheese sandwich and some of that leftover soup."

"That sounds good."

Tony slipped me a glass of milk and then returned to the refrigerator to gather items for our lunch.

"I spoke to Dad about a name for the baby," I said.

"Did you? What did he think?"

"He liked the names we've decided on and agreed that a nickname was a good idea. When I told him that one of the nicknames we were considering was Tommi, he told me that my grandmother went by Tommy, but it was spelled with a 'y.'"

Tony stopped what he was doing. "Your real grandmother?"

I nodded. "That's what Dad said. He revealed that his mother's name was Thomasina, which was the primary influence in his decision to choose Thomas as his alias when he elected to settle down and start a family. He also shared that she was a tiny little spitfire who everyone called Tommy. I told him I would love to name our baby after the grandmother I'd never known, and he said he thought she would be honored."

Tony smiled. "I guess we have our name and our nickname."

I smiled back. "I guess we do. I still think I want to spell Tommi with an 'i,' but I love that this woman who is long dead and I'll never meet can still have a place in our lives."

"I'm somewhat surprised your dad told you what he did."

"I don't think he meant to. I think it slipped out when I mentioned that Tommi was one of the nicknames being considered. He did say that telling me was probably a bad idea and that we should keep it between us. I explained that I would tell you but no one else and told him I thought he should tell Mike. He indicated that he would."

"Did he mention anything else?" Tony asked as he placed the buttered bread on the griddle.

"Not really. I asked about my grandfather, but Dad said he died before he was born, and he never knew his name. He also said that his mother died when he was young, but he clammed up when I asked who raised him."

"I'm not surprised. I guess one of the frustrations with having your father in your life is that there are parts of his past that none of us will likely ever know about."

"I guess that's true." I laughed. "Honestly, I'm not even sure what he told me today is true. I think the part about Tommy being his mother's nickname is true. That was all very spontaneous. It was almost like he said what he did before realizing what he was saying. The part about never knowing his father and his mother dying when he was young seemed a bit more calculated. I asked a question, and he took his time answering. If I find out that part isn't true, I won't be surprised, but as you indicated, maybe it doesn't really matter. He's in our lives now, and he has a whole new identity, which we all need to learn to use when speaking to or talking about him. It will only take one slip of the tongue to undo everything he has worked for."

"If you slip and call him Dad in front of someone else, I guess that could lead to questions that might lead to suspicion."

"Exactly. I must stop calling my dad 'Dad' even when we're alone. He's Hank now, and he needs to be Hank all the time, not just in certain situations, the same way that Sam is Sam all the time."

"Of course, we didn't know Sam before he was Sam, so it was easier not to slip up."

"True. But this is crucial, so I need to try twice as hard to get it right."

While we ate, Tony shared his plan to head into town and do some errands after our meal. He asked me if I wanted to go with him or stay home and rest, and I indicated that I'd enjoy some time away from the house. His first stop would be the town offices to attempt to fix a couple errors on the permits we needed for the craft fair and the kiddie carnival. I wasn't sure I wanted to do that, so I asked him to drop Tilly and me off at Hap's hardware and home supply store. It had been almost two weeks since I'd dropped in on Hap. Tilly and I were definitely overdue for a visit.

Chapter 10

"Tess, Tilly," Hap greeted when Tilly and I walked in from the street. "What a nice surprise. It's been a while."

"It has been a while," I agreed as Tilly trotted over to get the dog cookie Hap always had behind the counter for her. "Now that I'm pregnant and not working or volunteering at the shelter, I'm not in town nearly as often as I used to be. I've missed everyone."

"And everyone has missed you." Hap offered me a hard candy, which I took. "I imagine you and Tony must be quite occupied preparing for the upcoming festivities."

"We are," I said as I unwrapped the candy and popped it in my mouth. "Tim and Tom will arrive in town tomorrow. From what I understand, the plan is to film a short segment at the antique shop in Kalispell on Sunday and then tackle the Montrose Estate on Monday. They plan to move onto the theater on Tuesday."

"I thought they were going to do the theater first."

"They were, but they decided to switch things up when they found out about the recent murder. I haven't spoken to the men personally, but according to Tony, I think the segments they film at the antique shop and the Montrose Estate will be greatly abbreviated from what they first planned." I tossed my candy wrapper in the trash. "I guess that makes sense since there will be a lot more interest in the theater, so allocating most of the time there seems to be the logical choice."

"And the Stonewall Estate?"

"They plan to film there on Saturday night. Since it's an after-dark thing, I assume they'll take a day to set things up. I'm not sure how the men will divide their time once they've filmed the short segments, but it does seem like they've bitten off a lot."

Hap chuckled. "Seems they aren't the only ones to have bitten off a lot."

Hap had a point. Tony and I would be exhausted before the Halloween Festival was over.

"Tony's trying to handle things without anyone's help, but it is a lot," I admitted. "He's at the town offices trying to get mistakes on the permits for the craft fair and kiddie carnival straightened out. Once

106

he's done there, he plans to meet me here to pick up the hardware for the kiddie carnival booths, which he plans to erect a week from today."

"Hattie and I were talking about it, and we both feel that you and Tony deserve to have help with all of this. I suggested we talk to Tony about asking folks to help, but Hattie wanted to put out some feelers to confirm that we could round up the help we needed before making any promises to Tony. We chatted this morning, and things are looking good in terms of finding willing volunteers, so she planned to call Tony later today. Since the two of you are in town now, I'll see if she can get away from the bakeshop so we can chat in person."

"That would be wonderful," I said. "Even a few volunteers would take some of the pressure off Tony."

Hap took his cell phone out and made his call to Hattie. Having help would make all the difference to Tony's stress level. Tony and I hadn't wanted to chair the event and, given the fact that I was expecting, I would never have volunteered, but when the mayor agreed to have the fireworks display moved away from the lake near the animal shelter in exchange for our willingness to take over the annual event, I made the decision to go along with his plan.

"If I take over the construction of the booths and Hattie takes over the chili cookoff, then all we'll need to do is find someone to take over the craft fair, kiddie carnival, and parade. If we can accomplish that, then you and Tony can focus on the Ghost Therapists," Hap said after he hung up with Hattie.

"It's only a week until the festival," I pointed out.

"It is, but you and Tony have already done a lot of the planning, so it might not be all that hard to get someone to take over from here."

I put a hand on my stomach and gave it a rub.

"Is Kiwi kicking her mommy?" Hap chuckled.

"She is. We finally settled on a name, so I imagine we won't be calling her Kiwi any longer."

"That's wonderful. And what name did you decide on?"

"Antonella Thomas Marconi. We're going to call her Tommi spelled with an 'i.'" I explained the meaning behind each name, leaving out the part about finding out I'd had a grandmother nicknamed Tommy.

Hap and I continued to chat about babies and names until Tony arrived. Hattie arrived five minutes after Tony and provided the list of the volunteers she'd spoken with. Hattie agreed to call everyone we'd chosen and confirm their assignment once we decided on the right fit for each volunteer. With only a week until the festival, we needed to get everyone on board sooner rather than later.

After Hattie left to return to her bakeshop and get started on her phone calls, Tony began collecting the supplies on his list, and Hap and I trailed behind him.

"Any word on the Jake Black murder case?" Hap asked while Tony dug through a bin filled with random nuts and bolts.

"I'm not sure," Tony replied. "Mike had some leads to follow up on, but I haven't spoken to him since this morning. In terms of physical evidence left behind that might help him identify the killer, there really wasn't anything that stood out as being important."

"I heard from a few of my customers that there has been speculation that Jake's death might be related to O'Leary's murder in some way," Hap said.

"That is the rumor currently making the rounds," Tony agreed.

"Any truth to it?" Hap asked.

Tony shrugged. "I don't think anyone knows at this point."

"You were around back when the usher was stabbed to death," I said to Hap. "Do you remember anything about it?"

"Sure. Gavigan was a friend. Finding his body behind the screen like that sent the whole town into a tailspin. Not only had Gavigan been a good man a lot of folks knew and liked, but his death had been so violent. Folks had a hard time wrapping their heads around that."

"I suppose it must have been a hard thing to accept. Do you remember what sorts of theories were floating around?" I asked. "Theories as to who killed the man and why the murder was carried out in the manner in which it was?"

Hap cleared his throat. "Most thought the movie that had been playing that night had gotten folks riled up to the point where at least one person in the audience lost their mind and acted on impulse. I never really bought that. I'm not a huge fan of the horror genre, but I've seen a few slasher movies in my day, and I can honestly say that watching a slasher on the screen in no way caused me to want to start hacking my friends to death."

"I heard that there was a theory that the killer might have been on drugs," I said.

Hap lifted one shoulder.

Tony moved down the aisle to another bin. I asked Hap what other theories he remembered.

"Well, there was the one about the secret society."

"Secret society?" I asked.

"A group of wealthy men with political clout who ran things around here. I won't go so far as to say there was anything secret about the group. The men met and discussed ways to steer White Eagle development and politics in such a way as to benefit themselves. Seems like everyone knew what was going on, and likely still is, for that matter."

"So the theory was that one or more of these men killed the usher due to something he knew doesn't really sit right with you."

"Not really. It's true that those who have cash also have clout, but it's always been that way, and it likely always will be. I think most folks accept it for what it is."

"So what do you think did happen?" I asked.

"I'm not sure, but my favorite theory had to do with the insect infestation."

I quirked an eyebrow at Hap. "Insect infestation?"

"At the time of Gavigan's murder, some odd climate changes occurred that caused the insects in the area to go crazy. Not only did these little buggy creatures become more active, causing half the town to drown in a bug infestation, but some claimed to have been attacked by masses of flying and crawling insects. I guess this caused some folks to think that Gavigan had been completely overtaken by burrowing insects, which caused him to stab himself in an attempt to dig them out."

"That's crazy."

"It is, but folks were scared after one of their own was so brutally murdered. There didn't seem to be a well-accepted theory as to who might have killed the guy, so folks let their imaginations take over."

"So, which theory did you get behind?" I asked.

"Not the insects. That theory was just nuts. And not the secret society. Gavigan's murder was flashy and seemed orchestrated to make a point. If he was killed because he knew something, it's more likely that he would have been shot, much like Jake Black was."

"And the drug-crazed moviegoer?"

"I can't really get behind that either." Hap ran a hand over his chin. "No. Seems to me that Gavigan's murder was personal. It was carried out by someone who felt rage and needed an outlet. If it had been me investigating, I would have spent more time looking into the guy's personal life than the men in charge of the investigation at the time seemed to."

I agreed with that. The usher's murder did seem personal.

"Was O'Leary married?" I asked, figuring a murder based on jealousy might lead to twelve stab wounds.

"No. But there had been someone when Gavigan was younger. A relationship that hadn't worked out. I don't know all the details, but I remember him commenting about having his heart broken once and being unwilling to put himself out there again. Gavigan was a friendly sort. He had a lot of friends and an active social life, but I can't ever remember him dating."

"Did he have any enemies you can think of?" I asked as Tony continued to the next row of hardware.

"A few. It's hard to get through life without stepping on a few toes along the way."

"Did anyone hate him enough to kill him?"

Hap paused to think about my question and then shook his head. "Not that I can think of offhand. Gavigan wasn't an ambitious man. Back then, he had a series of low-paying jobs that didn't seem to be the sort of thing to put him into competition with anyone else."

"What sort of jobs?" I asked. "Other than the theater, of course."

"He worked nights and weekends at the theater, and he worked weekdays for a local grocer. The grocer he worked for has since closed, but it used to be owned by a family who'd run the place for generations. When Gavigan wasn't working, he'd stop by the bar and have a pint with friends. He seemed to enjoy playing chess in the park during the warmer months. He was a simple man with simple needs. I can't really put my finger on a motive for anyone to want to kill the man, but obviously, someone did."

"Had Gavigan lived here long before his death?"

Hap replied. "I guess about five or six years."

"And before that?"

He slowly shook his head. "No idea. Other than offering a failed relationship to explain why he wasn't interested in dating, he never really talked about his life before he moved to White Eagle."

"He sounds like a man running from something," I said. "Low profile jobs, low profile lifestyle, and casual friendships that likely didn't lend themselves to oversharing."

Hap agreed that low profile, low key, unremarkable, and fairly vanilla was a perfect description for Gavigan.

By the time Tony finished gathering his supplies, I was beginning to experience the midday slump I'd had to deal with since becoming pregnant, so Tony paid for the items he'd gathered, and then we headed home. We'd barely pulled into our drive when Mike called to let us know that Bree was in the hospital again and this time she was definitely having the baby. Tony let all the dogs out while I headed upstairs to wash up, and then Tony and I headed to the hospital to help welcome the newest member of our tribe into the family.

Chapter 11

By the time Tony and I arrived at the hospital, Mom and Sam were sitting in the waiting room with none other than the newest White Eagle resident, Hank Hannigan. I wasn't sure if I was surprised to see him there or if I had expected him to show up for Michael's birth. Both, I supposed, if that was even possible.

"Mom." I leaned in and gave her a kiss on the cheek. I turned toward the men. "Sam, Hank."

"I'm glad you made it in time," Mom said, seeming to be totally comfortable with the fact that she was sitting between her dead husband and one of his best friends, her current lover. "Mike spoke to the doctor, who thinks Bree's labor will be quick."

"I hope so, for Bree's sake. I take it Mike is in with her now."

Mom confirmed that he was, but she also mentioned that Mike had instructed her to have me go to the labor room once I arrived. I offered Tony an apologetic glance, leaving him with my unique family before heading to the nurses' station to check in.

"Tess Marconi. I'm here to visit Bree Thomas."

"Are you family?" the nurse asked.

"Best friend, sister-in-law, and labor coach."

The nurse smiled at me, glancing at my stomach as she did so. "I see you'll be on the other side of the birthing process in a few months."

I agreed that I would be, accepted the visitor's name tag she handed me, and headed down the hallway to labor room four.

"Oh good, you made it," Bree said, reaching out a hand to me. "This is going fast."

"That's great," I said.

"It is, but I need to catch my breath, and I feel like I need things to stop for just a minute." She let out a little screech as another contraction gripped her body.

"As long as you're here, I'm going to step out for a moment," Mike said.

It was apparent that Bree was preparing to protest this move, so Mike merely assured her he'd be quick and then slipped out the door.

"He's such a baby," Bree said. "You'd think a cop would handle things like a woman in labor a little better."

"I don't think it's that he can't handle the stress of a woman in labor. I think it's probably just hard for him to see the woman he loves in pain."

"Maybe, but he's had eyes on that doorway ever since the contractions started coming hard and fast." She gasped again, and I grabbed her hand.

I had to admit that while I was anxious to have my body back and was totally jazzed to meet my baby, I wasn't looking forward to this part of the process.

"Is your mom here?" Bree asked. "She was going to ask Laverne Grossman to watch Ella, and then she planned to come to the hospital, but Mike never told me if she made it."

"My mother and my father are both here," I answered.

"Your dad is here?"

"Well, technically, Hank came with Sam, who, as you know, is a friend from way back."

Bree bit down hard and rode out the next contraction. "This musical identity thing is getting ridiculous," she offered once the contraction passed. "First, Mike tells me that his dad is dead, and then he tells me that he isn't actually dead but is living under a different name. I finally wrap my head around that, and Uncle Garret suddenly arrives. It was an odd situation, but I'd finally make peace with the idea, only to have Uncle Garret metamorphous into Hank Hannigan right before my eyes."

"It has been a bit of a rollercoaster, but I think things will settle into a steady state now that Hank has arrived."

"Ella still calls your dad Dapa even though he looks like Hank and not the Dapa she was first introduced to."

I frowned. "Yeah. That could potentially be a problem. We may need to have a family meeting to discuss the situation at some point. At least Michael and Tommi will always know Hank as Hank."

"Tommi. Did you make a decision?"

"We did. Kiwi's name will be Antonella Thomas Marconi, more commonly known as Tommi, and as you suggested, it will be spelled with an 'i.'"

Bree smiled. "I love it. Have you told your mom?"

"Not yet, but I will. Today. So far, the only people I've told are you, Dad, Hap."

"You told Hap before me?"

I shrugged. "Tony and I were visiting with Hap and Hattie before we got the call to come here, and a name for the baby just came up in a conversation I had with Hap before Tony and Hattie joined us."

I could tell that Bree wasn't happy about not being told ahead of Hap, but at that moment, she had other things on her mind, and I doubted she'd even remember to be mad once Michael arrived. I did need to tell Mom, and I best do that today.

As promised, Mike came back into the room after a thirty-minute break. The doctor came in right behind him, so I returned to the waiting room, where Tony and the rest of the family were waiting.

"How's it going?" Mom asked.

"I think it will be soon. In fact, I won't be surprised if the doctor decides to move Bree to delivery."

"I just can't wait to meet my grandson," Mom said.

Dad reached over, took her hand, and gave it a squeeze. It was a friendly squeeze of support, but the whole thing struck me as odd.

I looked at Tony, sending him a meaningful glance. He nodded.

"Tony and I have decided on a name for our baby," I said.

"You have?" Mom clapped her hands together in anticipation.

"Antonella will be her first name. We chose that name to honor Nona, who meant so much to Tony as a child."

"That's a beautiful name," Mom said. "And very Italian."

"We thought so. I also wanted to honor my family, so her middle name will be Thomas."

There was a lot of oohing and ahhing at this point.

I continued. "Tony and I both wanted to settle on a nickname that was a bit more manageable than Antonella. Toni and Ella were taken, so we actually talked about this quite a lot, but after a conversation with Hank, we've decided to call her Tommi spelled with an 'i.'" I looked at Dad, who appeared to be more emotionally choked up than I remembered ever seeing him. Luckily, Mike wasn't here, and Mom didn't seem to notice Dad's eyes tear up. It was too bad that I couldn't tell Mom about Grandma Tommy, but I suspected that Dad had only shared that with me in a moment of weakness and was likely already regretting it.

"I should get back and check on Bree," I told the group. "Hopefully, it won't be long now."

Thankfully, we didn't have a long wait for Michael's arrival. Once Bree was moved to delivery, things went quickly, and Michael was nestled snuggly in his daddy's arms before the group in the waiting room had time to wonder how it was going.

"He's here," I informed the group when I returned. I had to suppress a gasp when I noticed that Aunt Ruthie had joined Tony, Mom, Sam, and Dad.

Aunt Ruthie had obviously known my father well. If anyone could penetrate his disguise, it would be someone like her or Hap. I glanced at Mom, who shook her head ever so slightly.

"When can we see him?" Tony asked.

"They're cleaning Bree up, and then an orderly or nurse will move her into a regular room. Once Bree and the baby are settled, Mike will come and get us," I answered.

I'd known from the beginning that Sam's friend and White Eagle's new resident, Hank Hannigan, would need to enter White Eagle society at some point. But, to be perfectly honest, I'd been terrified of this eventuality ever since I'd learned my father's plan to finally retire and be part of the lives of everyone he'd had to leave behind. Initially, the dynamics between Dad and Sam concerned me. Dad had sent Sam to look after Mom once Sam had decided to retire from the same black ops group Dad worked for, but over the years, Mom and Sam had become much more than neighbors. It must have been odd for Dad to see his wife and best friend together, yet, so far, it seemed that both men were handling things just fine.

After receiving the go-ahead, everyone followed Mike to Bree's room, where she was sitting in the bed holding her adorable son. Everyone oohed and ahhed over him, but after only a few minutes, Mike announced that Bree needed to rest, and he politely kicked us all out. Mom suggested that we go out to dinner to celebrate, which meant the stress of watching Aunt Ruthie with Dad would last a couple more hours. Although I was nervous that Dad would say or do something to give away his real identity, I supposed that Hank would have to be launched into White Eagle society at some point, so perhaps having Aunt Ruthie on hand for this test run wasn't the worst idea. If she didn't recognize him, it was unlikely that anyone else would either, but if she did, she loved us enough to keep his secret if we asked her to.

"I'm starving," I said as I watched Dad chatting with Sam over the top of my menu. Mom sat next to Sam, who sat next to Dad. All three sat across from Aunt Ruthie, Tony, and me. "I think I'll have a petite filet and a salad. My doctor wants to be sure I get enough protein."

I realized I was rambling, and I doubted anyone cared what I was going to order, but I was nervous about how this dinner was going, and I rambled when I was nervous.

"A steak sounds good," Hank seconded. "But I think I'll go with a New York cut and a baked potato."

I glanced at Aunt Ruthie, who was still studying her menu. She didn't appear to be any more aware of Hank than she would have been of anyone else she'd just met. Maybe this would work after all. Tony and I had discussed the significant risk involved with Dad retiring in White Eagle, where people were familiar with Grant Thomas. Sam was already retired when he moved here, and he hadn't been from here, so he arrived in town without the baggage created by previous relationships. I was sure that Dad's handlers had tried to talk him into settling down in a location he'd never visited as Grant Thomas or one of his other aliases, but he was determined to be part of his grandchildren's lives. I believe Mike, Mom, and I all wanted that for him.

Tony pulled his cell phone out of his pocket and looked down at the display. He glanced at me. "I need to take this. Just order the meatloaf special for me."

I asked if he wanted mashed potatoes or a substitute, and he responded that mashed potatoes were okay as he got up and headed toward the restaurant's front door.

"I guess that must have been important for Tony to leave like that," Aunt Ruthie said.

"I'm sure it was. Tony is usually good about not answering calls during dinner unless he's expecting an important call."

"He's helping Mike with the murder investigation," Mom pointed out. I loved that she was sticking up for Tony. She was usually the sort to make a fuss about cell phones at the dinner table, but she seemed to have mellowed since she'd found out the truth about Dad. I supposed that the way things had initially ended with him had been a heavy burden on her mind all this time.

"How's that going?" Aunt Ruthie asked.

My response was to simply say that while Mike and his team were working on it with Tony's help, they hadn't made any real breakthroughs the last time I'd spoken to Mike about the case.

When Tony returned to the table, Mom asked him if everything was okay. He said it was and then shared a problem we'd been having with the permits for the upcoming Halloween Festival. While he'd never directly said the call had been related to the festival, the way he introduced the subject led to that conclusion. Aunt Ruthie commented about the chili cookoff, and the subject of the festival, in general, took over. When Tony shared that Hap and Hattie had offered to help round up volunteers, Ruthie reached for the pen and small notepad she kept in her purse to start a list.

"It's been quite a day," Tony said as we drove back toward our home on the mountain.

"It really has," I agreed. "I almost fainted when I walked into the hospital to find Aunt Ruthie and Dad sitting not five feet from one another."

"I held my breath for a second or two when Ruthie arrived, too, but it seemed like everything went fine. I didn't notice that Ruthie paid more attention to Hank than she would have if any other friend of Sam's had come to the hospital with Mom and Sam."

"I agree." I blew out a long breath. "Maybe this is actually going to be okay."

Tony reached across the seat and squeezed my hand.

"By the way," I said. "Who was really on the other end of the call you took at the restaurant?"

"A man named Glen Price. I came across his name while digging into the backgrounds of Gavigan O'Leary and Jake Black. His name stood out because he actually knew both men."

"Did he? How did he know the men?"

"Glen worked at the theater in the snack bar when O'Leary was an usher. Glen was just out of high school and still trying to find his grove, so he had a lot of different jobs. I'm not sure how often Glen and O'Leary worked the same shift, but I found some photos of Glen and Gavigan together, and it appears they were close."

"And Jake?"

"Glen worked with Jake at the lumber mill until Jake disappeared. I called and spoke to their supervisor, who shared that the men were close and seemed to be into conspiracy theories and such. I guess they even went to Roswell, New Mexico, the summer before Jake disappeared, and according to the man I spoke to, both claimed to have spent time at Area 51 in Nevada."

"So both men were into the alien culture."

"Basically. Anyway, when I realized that Glen had known both victims, I called him and asked for an interview. Of course, he turned me down flat, claiming that he didn't talk to cops. I tried to assure him that I wasn't a cop, but in his mind, working with cops was the same as being a cop. I wasn't getting anywhere, so I asked Shaggy about the guy. It turns out that Shaggy and Glen are casual friends, so once Shaggy vouched for me, Glen decided to answer my questions. Shaggy persuaded Glen to meet with me tomorrow morning and offered the video game store as a safe and impartial venue."

"It was nice of Shaggy to get involved."

"Shaggy can be odd at times, but he's actually a really nice guy who cares about people and is just as interested as any of us in seeing justice served."

"What time are you meeting?"

"Eleven. If you want to visit with Bree and Michael, I can drop you off, but if you prefer to stay home and rest, that's perfectly fine with me."

"Are Tim and Tom still arriving tomorrow?" I asked.

"As far as I know. I don't know what time the Ghost Therapists plan to arrive, but they haven't asked for my help with anything so far. My plan is to focus on the Halloween Festival. Even if Hap and Hattie are successful in finding people to take over the oversight of the craft fair, parade, and kiddie carnival, it'll still be up to us to ensure that everyone actually does what they promise to do, so I'd like to stay on top of it."

"Next year, we'll stick to our guns about not being chairpersons again."

Tony smiled. "I was ready to stick to our guns this year."

I sighed. "I know. If it hadn't been about the safety and well-being of the animals at the shelter, I would have stuck to my guns as well."

Tony announced he was taking the dogs out, and then we'd head to bed. I went upstairs to wash up but couldn't help but pause at the nursery as I passed it. After nine long months, Bree finally had Michael in her arms. Two more months, and I'd have Tommi in mine.

Chapter 12

By the following Monday, life had settled into a regular ebb and flow. Mike had brought Bree and Michael home from the hospital, and both mom and baby were doing well. Mike shared with me that while he was still committed to tracking down Jake's killer, he didn't feel the passion for the hunt that he usually did. In fact, he was so obsessed with spending time with his new son that he'd all but turned the investigation over to Frank and Gage while he supervised in the background. Unfortunately, Frank and Gage weren't really getting anywhere. Tony was helping where he could, including meeting with Glen Price on Saturday, but the meeting hadn't yielded any significant insights. Tony suspected Glen was holding something back, so Shaggy agreed to work on him, but in the meantime, he seemed to be at a dead end. As for me, I was more than happy to pitch in with theory building, but as was the norm with cases that never got solved, I wasn't getting anywhere either.

On another note, Tim and Tom were in town. They'd visited Nancy at the antique store in Kalispell yesterday. After spending three hours with the Gentlemen's Chest, they finally informed her that the chest of drawers was not only currently free of ghosts, but they were pretty sure it had never housed a ghost. I spoke to her on the phone, and I could tell she was disappointed, but she didn't seem mad that her shop wouldn't be featured on their show as she hoped. In fact, she apologized to me for wasting everyone's time. After they left Kalispell, it was still early in the day, so Tim and Tom headed to the Montrose Estate. After a couple hours, they determined that the Montrose Estate was as ghostless as Nancy's chest of drawers. I sympathized with Nancy and Hannah, but I suspected that Tim and Tom were excited about getting started at the theater and hadn't put as much into the ghost hunt at the antique store or the mansion as they otherwise might have.

Tony and I planned to meet the men at the theater today, which I was excited about. Out of all the properties they'd started with, I thought this property held the most potential.

After we met with Tim and Tom, we planned to meet with Hap and Hattie. They'd worked hard this weekend and had managed to arrange a meeting between Tony and me and the newly appointed chairperson of each of the Halloween Festival's events. Hattie had successfully found someone to oversee the parade, which consisted of a group of children dressed in costumes who walked down Main Street. I was happy that I didn't have to worry about getting everyone organized and even happier that I didn't have to worry about the setup and judging of the chili cookoff, which Hattie was still planning to oversee.

"It looks like Shaggy's here," Tony announced after a vehicle pulled into the drive, and he looked out the window.

"Were you expecting him?"

"He said he might stop by to use my computers, but I didn't realize he planned to come by this early. On the days he works from the clean room, he usually stops by the video game store first to confirm that all his staff members have shown up and that everyone has what they need."

"Maybe he had more to do today than usual and wanted to start early."

"Maybe." Tony walked toward the front door and opened it before Shaggy even knocked. He greeted Shaggy and Buddy and then offered Shaggy a cup of coffee while his dog said hi to our dogs.

"You're getting an early start today," Tony said as he handed Shaggy a mug of coffee.

"I wanted to catch you before you left for the day. I have news."

"What sort of news?" Tony asked, offering him a seat.

Shaggy sat down at the kitchen table across from me. "I told you I was going to go back and listen to the Jake Black podcasts I missed while we were working on the game, which I have done. I also relistened to the podcasts I listened to in the background while working on other things, and hadn't given my full attention the first time around. My memory had been correct. Jake had developed an obsession with Gavigan O'Leary's death shortly before his own demise. I remember thinking that it didn't seem in the best interest of the podcast to spend so much time carrying on about a murder that happened a quarter century ago when there were a lot of current conspiracies that he might have addressed. Jake was the sort to care more about his interest in the content of his podcasts than he was in listeners' interest, so he usually talked about his compulsion of the moment."

Tony and I already knew this much, but Shaggy seemed to be working up to something, so we just waited for him to continue.

"While listening to a podcast taped just days before Jake's death, I realized he had referred to something I was sure he hadn't spoken about in a previous podcast. This caused me to wonder if Jake didn't have more than one outlet for his conspiracy theories, so I did some digging."

"You found something?" Tony asked.

"I did. The podcast I've been referring to all along is a mainstream podcast, at least amongst conspiracy theorists, and is readily available for listening via a free subscription through the usual channels. After a few dozen hours of digging, I found a second podcast, which is only accessible to those with access to the dark web. This second podcast typically delved into the types of modern-day conspiracies that might get a person killed or arrested if the wrong person found out about what was being discussed."

"So we're talking about conspiracies involving high-ranking politicians, the commitment of a crime, or interactions with well-connected criminals," I said.

"Basically. The limited access podcast Jake produced was geared toward hardcore conspiracists who tend to go the extra mile and put legs to their theories and beliefs."

"So we're talking the folks who camp out in the desert and wait for aliens," I said.

"That would be one group who might find a community of other people who share their passion and are willing to physically take action." Shaggy agreed. "Based on a sampling of Jake's most recent interactions, it seems that he was most interested in the story of Buford Stonewall, his fortune in stolen gold, his trip west, and his rise in political power."

"Wait, stolen gold?" I asked. "I thought Buford found gold."

"Not according to Jake. Jake believed the gold was stolen from a powerful crime family and then brought west when Buford ran. Jake also believed that much of the gold Stonewall brought west is still hidden somewhere on the Stonewall property."

I supposed that might explain why none of the cousins were willing to settle for less than they might otherwise end up with if they hung in until the end and why they were unwilling to sell the property and divide the cash. "Okay, say that's true. How does a fortune in gold hidden somewhere on the Stonewall Estate lead to the death of Gavigan O'Leary in the theater?"

"I'm not sure yet," Shaggy admitted. "That part doesn't really fit at this point, but what does fit is the idea that if there actually is a cache of gold somewhere, and Jake was actively talking about it to his compadres, that sort of speculation might have gotten him killed."

"I guess I can see how the potential heirs might have done whatever it took to stop Jake from running his mouth about a stash of gold they were all looking for," I said. "If his discussion of the gold with his conspiracy theory buddies is what got him killed, then the fact that he happened to have been killed in the theater might not be related to his research into O'Leary's death at all."

"I suppose it's possible that Jake's death had nothing to do with his reason for being in the theater, and solving his murder may not help us to solve O'Leary's as we hoped," Tony agreed.

While the idea of stolen gold hidden on the Stonewall Estate seemed like a good motive to pursue, I really had no idea what to do with that information, and Tony and I were overloaded this week with Tim and Tom's presence in town and the opening of the Halloween Festival on Friday evening.

Tony suggested we stop by Mike and Bree's house and talk to Mike about Shaggy's idea, which made sense to me. We decided to leave all the dogs with Shaggy today, so Tony and I quietly snuck out when Tilly wasn't watching.

I was about to ring the bell next to Mike and Bree's front door when Bree opened the door before I could press the button.

"Michael's sleeping," she whispered. "Finally. He had a rough night, so I don't want to wake him."

"Of course." I lowered my hand. "We'll be quiet. Is everything okay?" I'd already begun to have nightmares about a baby who wouldn't stop crying.

"Everything is fine. I think we're all just trying to find our groove. Michael loves to be held, even more than Ella used to, but when you try to put him down, he screams. Mike says we need to ignore the cries, and I know he's right, but he's only a few days old. It's hard to just stand by and listen to him wail."

"I guess it would be a bit of a shock to go from being safe and sound in Mommy's belly to all on your own in the cold, bright world. I don't think there's anything wrong with giving him time to adjust."

"I agree. But I need to sleep, so Michael needs to make peace with his crib. Can I get you some coffee? Decaf?"

"No," I answered. "I'm good. Maybe you should go and take a nap while the baby is sleeping."

"I think I might. I hate to desert you."

"I'm fine. Tony and I have a full day, so we can't stay long. I'll head into the living room and listen in while Tony catches Mike up."

Bree gave me a hug and headed up to bed. I headed into the living room and quietly listened while Tony shared the second podcast that Shaggy had found and the potential ramifications.

Mike took a moment to reel it all in before he finally spoke. "Okay, let me see if I have this right. Jake claimed that part of the gold Buford brought to Montana with him at the turn of the century has been hidden on the estate." He paused and then continued. "I guess I can buy that as being a possibility. It's no secret that Buford came west with the gold he found or possibly stole. Everyone knows that when Buford arrived, he had a lot of cash and bought a ton of land. Land was cheap back then, so he wouldn't have needed a lot of gold to buy what he did. I suppose if his personal wealth without the gold grew to the point where he no longer needed to use the gold as currency, he might have stashed it somewhere." Mike paused again. "It seems likely that he would have told his heir where the gold was hidden and how to access it. I can't think of a reason for him to take the secret to his grave. On the one hand, if that's the case, and each heir had access to the gold, then it seems likely that it might be gone by now, even if Buford stashed it away at some point."

Tony and I both agreed that Mike's logic made sense so far.

"On the other hand," Mike continued, "if the gold still exists, or even if the legend of the gold exists, and there are people out there who believe it exists, I can see the lure of riches being a viable motive for murder. I suppose there are those, such as the cousins, who figure that the gold belongs to them and wouldn't take kindly to others snooping around."

"So perhaps one of the cousins found out about the gold and told the others," I said. "Or maybe the cousin who found out didn't tell the others but took care of things on his or her own."

"That seems like a decent theory," Mike said. He frowned. "I'm still not sure about the logic behind allowing the settlement of the estate to drag on and on the way it has." He looked directly at Tony. "I think I'm going to see if I can convince the attorney in charge of the whole thing to have a conversation with me. I don't have enough to force the issue if he's unwilling to tell me what he knows about the situation, but I figure I have a reason now to at least try."

"Or maybe Tim and Tom will be successful in their bid to speak to the ghost living in the mansion, and perhaps we can learn the rest of the story that way," I said to Mike.

He just smiled.

Tony jumped back in. "While the fact that Jake was talking about the gold is an interesting aspect of this whole thing and may well provide a motive for the murder, I also think we need to keep in mind that Jake was at the theater to investigate something having to do with Gavigan O'Leary. While a fortune in gold sounds about as good a motive as any I've heard, the gold is purported to be hidden at the Stonewall Estate. There isn't an obvious reason for Jake to have been at the theater unless he was looking for something to support his theory about how O'Leary died."

"Jake thought someone with a political connection killed O'Leary," Mike confirmed.

"That seemed to be his favorite theory. Or at least it was the theory he talked about the most in his podcast."

Mike frowned. "Twelve stab wounds don't sound like a killing of necessity. It sounds like a killing of passion."

Tony and I agreed that we felt the same way and had said as much on several occasions, yet it was also true that Jake seemed to spend a lot of time talking about the political connection.

"Maybe the political connection as a motive for O'Leary's murder was a decoy," Mike said.

"Decoy?" I asked.

"Keep in mind that Jake Black didn't trust anyone. He saw lies everywhere he looked. It makes sense that if he was going to talk to the public, at large, about something important to him, he might twist things a bit to keep those he felt unworthy of the truth from finding out what that truth might be."

Mike made a good point. It sounded like Jake was the sort who saw a conspiracy everywhere he looked. Had he made up the part about the political motive to divert his listeners from finding out the real reason he was so interested in a murder that occurred a quarter of a century ago?

"If that's the case, what is his real agenda?" I asked. "The gold? Do you think Jake actually believed the gold had been hidden in that old building rather than on the estate as he claimed during his podcast?"

Mike just shrugged. "The theater didn't exist when Buford died, but by the time O'Leary was stabbed to death, the building was owned by a Stonewall who might have moved it from the estate for some reason."

Tony looked at his watch. "We need to go. We're supposed to meet up with Tim and Tom in thirty minutes, and I need to stop and pick up the key. I'll have my cell phone if you figure anything out. Maybe we can talk later."

"Call me later," Mike said. "If Bree and Michael are doing okay, maybe you can pick up takeout and swing back by. I should have an update from Frank and Gage by the end of the day."

Chapter 13

Tim and Tom were waiting for us at the theater when we arrived. Our only task today was to show them around and answer any questions they may have. Tony had put in some time researching both murders that occurred in the building, so while we might not be able to answer all their questions, he had a rudimentary background to share. Tony suggested that I wait outside, but I wanted to be inside where the action was, so I countered with my intention to follow them into the main seating area of the theater as I had before and to wait there. The trip into the interior took longer than it had when Tony and I had come alone. Tim and Tom not only paused to speak to each other every few steps, but they also paused to ask Tony questions.

I had to admit that the men seemed excited about the venue. The men felt there were indicators of ghostly energy, although they conceded that it was too early to tell whose energy they were picking up on. As the men exchanged ideas about the setup locations and the optimal time for filming, their enthusiasm was infectious, and I couldn't help but get swept up in their excitement.

We'd been inside the dark theater for at least thirty minutes by the time we'd made our way to the stage, where the screen hung at an angle. Tony cautioned the men that the area behind the screen was strewn with debris and that they'd need to tread carefully to avoid a fall. As I'd indicated to Tony that I would, I turned around to head back down the aisle to the lobby. I supposed I'd wait outside since the theater was cold and drafty, and the sunshine outside sounded darn good. I'd made my way about halfway back up the center aisle, heading toward the lobby, when something ran past me, brushing my leg. Of course, the ensuing gasp was inevitable and couldn't be prevented after having just spent the past half hour talking to the Ghost Therapists about ghosts in the building. Once my heart stopped pounding, I stopped walking and looked around. I wasn't sure I even believed in ghosts, but I'd definitely felt something brush my leg. Using my flashlight, I slowly scanned the room. I didn't see anything, but I supposed a ghost might be felt and not seen. Then I heard a tiny little cry that sounded like it was coming from somewhere beyond the stage's perimeter.

I hesitated, trying to decide what to do. Tony wouldn't want me wandering around the theater alone, but I was curious about the cry. I could call and ask him to come back and check it out, but I knew he was busy with Tim and Tom, and I hated to bother the men if I'd just imagined the whole thing.

Then I heard the cry again. I took a step forward and slowly made my way down the aisle. After each step, I paused and listened, but it seemed that whatever had been making the noise I'd heard had moved on.

"Okay," I said to myself, mumbling under my breath. "Ghost or animal?"

Did ghosts even make noises? The stereotypical ghost floated around the space they haunted, making a boo sort of noise. But most of the ghost shows I'd watched on TV featured ghosts that were seen or experienced through their interactions with the physical objects in a space they occupied but were never heard.

I stood entirely still and listened for the sound, but whatever I'd been hearing before appeared to be gone now. There was a cold breeze coming from somewhere, and I'd left my sweater in the truck, so I decided to do the responsible thing for Tommi and me, and I obediently turned around and headed back to our vehicle.

When I stepped out of the cold, dark theater into the brilliant sunshine, I paused to enjoy the warmth on my shoulders. The wind had picked up since we'd been here, so I continued to the truck to retrieve my sweater. Once I had that, I decided to walk around to the back of the building. The theater was built on an isolated piece of land with the highway in front of it and a deep gully behind it. Rolling hills were beyond the gully, and I was sure the view would be fabulous. Tony texted to let me know that the men wanted to explore the catwalk and that he'd be a few more minutes, so I decided to walk around the building to get a better view of the scenery created where the gully met the hillside.

That was when I saw the cat. A tiny gray and white cat, who, based on the sagging nipples, had recently given birth.

"Hey, there," I said to the cat. "Are you here all alone?"

"Meow."

I looked around. "It looks as if you have babies somewhere. If you show me where they are, I can help you move them to a safer place."

The cat appeared to be listening to me. I didn't want to scare the cat away, so I slowly moved forward, speaking softly and calmly as I approached. When I was about five feet away, the cat turned and disappeared into a crack in the exterior wall. The crack was barely wide enough for the cat to get through, so it wasn't as if I was going to be able to follow. I'd placed my flashlight in my sweater's pocket when I'd put it on, so I very carefully lowered myself to the ground, shone the light into the gap the cat had disappeared into, and tried to see what sort of space existed beyond the exterior wall.

The space where the mama cat and her babies had nested was small, but I supposed it was adequate for their needs. There was another wall behind the space, although based on my limited view, it appeared to be temporary rather than a permanent interior wall. I could see a space beneath the wall that looked to have been tacked into place. The gap was maybe six inches to a foot in height. It was hard to tell from my vantage point. I didn't suppose the height of the gap mattered as much as getting the mama and babies to safety. But how?

I slowly stood up. Pushing my hands into my back, I allowed my body a moment to recover before deciding on my next move.

The building's exterior wall was stucco. The crack the cat had slipped through was likely the result of a geographic or weather-related incident that caused the exterior walls to shift and the gap to appear. The only way to get the cat and kittens out through the exterior wall would be to cut a hole in the side of the building. I supposed it wasn't an entirely unreasonable idea, but I'd need permission to alter the structure, which would take time.

The other option would be to find the temporary interior wall and go in that way. That made more sense, but I'd need a plan that allowed someone to cut through the wall while a second person waited outside should the mother try to escape that way. I'd also need a way to ensure that I was able to catch the mother once she was out and that I had some way to transport the mama and babies once I had them. I needed a trap and a crate. I needed Aspen.

Taking my cell phone out, I called her number.

"Hey, Tess. What's up? Are you in town?"

"Actually, I'm out at the old movie theater." I went on and explained the situation and the help I needed.

"I'll grab what we need and be there in twenty minutes. Hopefully, the mama cat will stay put in the meantime."

"Hopefully. I'm going to wait here near the opening of the exterior wall. I'll know if the mama cat leaves. If she slips under the fake interior wall into the interior of the building, we'll track her down."

Once Aspen promised to hurry and hung up to collect the necessary supplies and equipment, I called Tony.

"Is everything okay?" he asked.

"Everything is fine," I said. I explained about the feline family. "Do you have tools in the truck that can create an opening large enough in the interior wall to fit through?"

"I do. Where exactly is this wall?"

"I'm outside, so I'm not exactly sure, but I think it's at the back of the building to the east. If I had to guess, I'd say that if you stand just behind the screen, face the rear of the building, and then look to your right, you'll see it. You'll feel a draft. The wind has really picked up, and the draft coming from the exterior crack can be felt even when you're inside. I felt it before I came outside."

"Okay, I'll finish here and then go and look for your wall."

"Based on what I can see from my side, it's a temporary wall that doesn't quite reach the floor. It looks like the sort of thing someone might have tacked up to create a partition."

"Okay. Stay put, and I'll call you back."

Aspen showed up just as Tony called to let me know he'd found the wall I was talking about. I asked Tony to wait where he was to make sure the cat didn't escape into the building until Aspen got there with the crate. Once Aspen had made her way to me, she looked at the feline family, and we'd discussed the best options to catch the mama cat before she fled. Aspen left the trap with me, and then she took the crate, some food, and a net and headed inside.

I set the trap up next to the exterior crack in the wall. If the mama cat decided to flee once Tony began to remove a section of the interior wall, she'd flee right into the trap. Aspen hoped to use the food and lures she had to get the mama cat to cooperate so we wouldn't need to go that route. Tony would slowly work the access to the space where the cats were nesting while Aspen was prepared to use the net if necessary.

As it turned out, the mama cat seemed happy to be rescued. Tony opened the wall, and Aspen reached in for the mama cat. Once she had her in the crate lined with a soft blanket, Aspen moved the kittens one at a time from the nest to the crate. When that was accomplished, she called out to let me know that she had the entire family and that she and Tony would be making their way out in a few minutes. I got down on my hands and knees and shone my light into the now-empty nest to confirm Aspen had everyone. That was when I noticed the reflection from the blade.

"Wait," I called out.

"Something wrong?" Aspen called back. "Did we miss a kitten?"

"No, not a kitten. But I do see something. It looks like a knife."

This time, it was Tony who called out. "I'm going to help Aspen move the cat family out to her vehicle so she can get them to the shelter and settled. Then I'll go back inside and grab the knife."

That sounded like a good plan to me. If the knife in the small space between the two walls was the knife that had killed Gavigan O'Leary, then it had been hidden in the space for a quarter century, so surely another few minutes wouldn't matter.

Chapter 14

Once Aspen had left to take the cat family to the shelter, Tony checked in with Tim and Tom one last time while I called Mike to let him know we had found a dusty old knife covered in a dark residue, which I assumed was blood, in the theater. It was hard to say how the knife ended up where it did. If the wall had already been in place when O'Leary was stabbed, assuming the knife did end up being the knife that had killed O'Leary, then my best guess was that the murder weapon had been dropped, and once dropped, it bounced and slid under the opening at the bottom of the wall. Either the killer didn't have time to look for it, or he didn't know where it had ended up, and the knife had simply been in the small space between the two walls until we found it today. I wasn't sure if the recovery of the knife, even if it turned out to be the knife that killed the usher, would lead to the identity of O'Leary's killer, but having the murder weapon could only help Mike in his attempt to solve the cold case.

"It seems likely to me that Jake somehow knew about the knife and had gone to the theater the night he died to look for it," I said to Mike once Tony and I arrived at his office, and we'd all gathered to discuss the case.

"Perhaps. Although, unless the killer told someone that he'd dropped the knife, had been unable to find it, and was forced to leave it behind, how would Jake ever know to look for it?" Mike countered.

"Maybe the killer did tell him," I said. "Before his death, Jake had become obsessed with the Gavigan O'Leary murder and had been dedicating his podcast to the theories that circulated at the time. Maybe the killer was a listener who simply couldn't help himself and responded."

"The responses are anonymous," Tony said. "Or the only thing that shows up when a response is made is the username, which is almost always something other than an individual's actual name."

"So the killer is following both the podcast and the discussion, and he decided to share a juicy tidbit from the safety of anonymity. The killer tells Jake about the knife, and Jake decides to go and look for it," Frank, who had joined in on the conversation, said. "Does that mean that when the killer realized that Jake planned to go and look for the knife, he realized his mistake and shot him?"

"Maybe," Mike said. "At this point, our best course of action is to look at the discussion that began after the podcast aired. If our theory is correct, we should be able to find the comment that shared the inside information about the knife. Once we have a username, Tony can backtrack and try to match a real person with the online persona."

It sounded as if Mike had a good plan. Tony and I were supposed to meet with Hap and Hattie and the rest of the new volunteers Hattie had dug up at the community center in less than fifteen minutes, so we arranged to meet up with Mike later in the day. He suggested we stop by the house around dinner time. Bree would enjoy the company, and they could work on the mystery in a comfortable setting. Tony offered to bring food, and we agreed to meet at five-thirty.

"Afternoon, Hap," I said after Tony and I wandered into the community center from the parking area. "Hattie," I said to include his lovely wife. "Are we early?" I asked after noticing that no one other than Hap and Hattie were present.

"A few minutes, but folks are running late. Connie Fallon volunteered to oversee the kiddie carnival, but her dental appointment ran late. She texted to let me know she'd be about fifteen minutes late but that she'd be here. I'll be taking over the chili cookoff," Hattie answered. "And I'm all set to do that. I even have my judges confirmed."

"That's great," I said. "Tony and I truly appreciate all you've done to pitch in."

"I don't mind. I enjoy the chili cookoff and have entered in the past, but I'd already decided not to enter this year, so doing the oversight isn't a conflict."

"And the parade?"

"Alberta Rosewood will tackle the parade, and Sue Wade will oversee the craft fair. Things really are handled. You and Tony can focus all your time on the *Ghost Therapy* filming and leave the rest to us."

I stepped forward and gave Hattie a good, hard hug. "Thank you. Really. You have no idea how much stress alleviates."

Hattie chuckled and patted my belly. "I think I do. I may not have been blessed with children, but I've been around enough expectant mothers to know that everyday tasks can become taxing when you're expecting. Hap tells me that you've settled on a name."

"We have." I then took a few minutes to fill Hattie in on the journey Tony and I had taken to come up with that name while we waited for the other chairwomen to arrive.

The actual meeting didn't take long at all. Everyone gave an update to the group on the project they were overseeing, a few questions were asked, suggestions were offered, and then everyone left to return to their jobs or businesses. The relief I felt knowing that Tony and I didn't have to worry about all those little details was considerable. I knew we'd promised to stop by Mike and Bree's later, but I really wanted to go home and take a long nap.

Instead, Tony and I decided to go by the shelter and check in with Aspen. I was sure the mama cat and kittens were fine, but it would soothe my mind to see them resting comfortably for myself. Besides, I hadn't had time to stop and chat with Brady for weeks. It would be good to catch up if he was between patients.

"Mama and babies all appear to be settling in nicely," Aspen said after leading me to the nursery. "Mama seems comfortable with human handling, so I suspect she was recently abandoned rather than feral. She may have even wandered away from her home, so I've posted found cat notices in all the usual places. If someone shows up to claim her, we'll do a screening and home visit to ensure that neglect wasn't involved with the cat wandering away. If the family is cleared, we'll turn the feline family over to their owners. If we don't get a response to our notices, or the family who tries to claim the cats seem unfit, we'll place the family with a foster until the kittens are old enough to be rehomed."

Of course, I already knew all of this since it was a policy I'd put in place, but it was good to hear that Aspen, who was now in charge of the shelter, had kept many of the practices I'd established.

"That all sounds perfect," I said. "And how are the bear cubs you took custody of a few weeks ago?"

"Settling in nicely. Would you like to see the bear cubs?"

"I would."

Tony had wandered off to call Shaggy when we arrived. He said something about sitting on the bench next to the small pond that had been added to the property for doggy playtime, but I didn't see him sitting there now, so he must have wandered in another direction.

"How is it working out with the dogs and the pond?" I asked as we passed by on our way to the bear habitat.

"So far, so good. Not all the dogs like the pond, but the fenced area is large enough for those who prefer to run around and play on the grass rather than venturing into the water. We have two to three volunteers in the play area with the dogs at any one time, and there are balls and ropes to throw, which our more energetic dogs seem to love."

"And when it snows?"

"The play area will still be accessed. Most dogs don't mind the snow. We plan to drain the pond in the winter to avoid anyone falling through the ice. This will be our first winter with the play area, so I'm anxious to see how it all works out."

"Do all the dogs have pond time and playtime?"

"We have a few dogs who prefer the company of humans to other dogs, so we're still matching volunteers to dogs for walking and training sessions." She punched a code in and opened a heavy steel door that led into the bear habitat. "By the way, you should talk to Brady before you leave. He said something about borrowing Kody for some search and rescue training."

"I'm sure Kody would love to train with Brady." I rubbed my stomach. "It looks like I won't be doing any S&R work for quite a while, so Brady should feel free to borrow Kody as often as he wants to."

"That's what I figured."

We entered the area that had been made to replicate the surrounding forest. There were two sections, one for young cubs and the other for older cubs and fully grown bears. Aspen had special training in wild animal rescue and rehabilitation, so agencies from miles around tended to call us when they had an injured bear or cub to place. Before her time in White Eagle, Aspen had previously worked for Zoe Donovan-Zimmerman, the owner of Zoe's Zoo. Widely regarded as the monarch of wild animal rescue and rehabilitation, Zoe's expertise was renowned; however, Aspen, a dedicated student, was cultivating a distinguished reputation in the field.

"It looks like we found Tony," Aspen said after we'd viewed the new cubs and then entered the core part of the habitat. Brady had tranquilized one of the older cubs, and Tony was helping to move him into the exam room.

"Is Glacier okay?" Aspen asked about the year-and-a-half-old cub as we joined the men in the room.

"She got into a scuffle with Henderson," Brady answered.

Henderson was a two-year-old cub who had come to us with a broken leg. He'd healed nicely, and both cubs were set to be released into the wild in a few weeks.

"I thought they were getting along," Aspen said.

Brady wiped the blood from a little scrape across Glacier's face. "They were, but I think both bears are feeling the call of the wild. Once I've thoroughly examined both bears to confirm that there's no major damage, I plan to call the forest service about releasing them sooner than the original date we'd settled on."

"If they don't want to move both release dates up, put a little pressure on them about Henderson, who truly is ready to go," Aspen suggested.

Brady asked me about the baby as he worked. I provided an update. I brought up the subject of Kody and assured him that it was okay to borrow him whenever he wanted or needed to. Kody was a trained search and rescue dog, and I was supposed to be his handler, but given recent developments, it didn't appear that I would be going out on rescues anytime soon. It was a shame to let the dog's skills go to waste, and I was happy that Brady wanted to pick up with him where I'd left off.

Tony and Brady had segued into a fishing conversation, so Aspen and I left them to their discussion, and we made our way to the small animal section of the wild animal unit. Currently in residence were four raccoons, three squirrels, a cotton-tailed bunny, and a skunk. Sometimes, when I visited the shelter, I felt sad that the dream of a wild animal unit as part of our operation had become a reality after I'd left. Not that I wasn't happy with my life and how it was progressing, but it would have been fun to be around more often as the shelter Brady and I had nurtured from the beginning began to find its legs.

"So, on a personal note, how are things with Brady?" I asked Aspen as she led me to the large cat area under construction.

She grinned. "So good. I'm so glad you pushed me to go for it. If you hadn't, Brady and I might have forever been stuck in a state of romance stasis."

I laughed. "Happy to help. I get why Brady, as your boss, was hesitant to make the first move, and I get why you, as an employee, were hesitant to make the first move with your boss, but anyone with eyes could see that the two of you were meant to be together. I'm so glad it's working out."

"Me too." She hugged me. "And thanks again. I owe you."

"Just invite me to the wedding."

She blushed. "We're not there yet, but if we get there, I want you to be my maid of honor."

Aspen and I continued chatting until Tony wandered over and suggested we head out. We still needed to pick food up to bring to Mike and Bree's, and Tony wanted to grab something a little more nutritious than regular takeout, so he suggested picking up the ingredients to make something easy. Tony was the best cook I'd ever met, so I knew that easy would be delicious.

Chapter 15

Mike, Bree, and I sat at the kitchen counter, sipping our beverages of choice as Tony made a nutritious and delicious-looking dish consisting of fresh veggies, penne pasta, and a red sauce he promised would bring the whole thing together.

"So update us on the knife, Mike," I requested after tasting the nonalcoholic sangria Tony had made for Bree and me.

"We managed to pull a fingerprint but don't have a match yet. The lab is working on it. The blood on the knife is also being tested. If Gavigan O'Leary had DNA on file somewhere, there's a good chance we'll find a match. It would be nice to confirm that we are dealing with the knife that killed the man."

"It might be hard to find a match for either the fingerprint or the blood," I said. "Gavigan O'Leary died twenty-four years ago."

"That's true," Mike said. "But I think we still have a good chance of finding a match for the fingerprint. It's the DNA that might be tough. If we can't find a match for the fingerprint or a direct DNA match for O'Leary, we'll try to find a familial match and back into an ID that way."

"Okay, wait," Bree said. "I feel like I missed a lot. Can someone catch me up?"

I shared the story of the mama cat and kittens and how the knife was found after rescuing them. Tony shared the fact that Jake Black appeared to have died after he went to the theater to look for something. Initially, we'd thought he was after the gold, but based on other data we'd uncovered, it appeared that the something he'd gone to look for was actually the knife that had killed Gavigan. I took over and shared that if we had the knife that killed O'Leary, that could provide not only a clue that would help us identify O'Leary's killer but a motive for Jake to have been killed as well.

"Motive?" Bree asked.

I responded. "The current theory is that Jake was shot in the head because he publicly stated that he knew about the missing knife and planned to look for it. We still need to verify this, but Tony and Shaggy are reviewing podcasts to see if he ever mentioned the knife. If he mentioned the knife specifically, then the killer, assuming he is still alive, might have decided it was a good idea to stop him from finding it."

"At this point, this is all speculation," I said. "But the idea that Jake was in the theater to find the knife when he was shot seems like a good avenue of investigation."

"Okay. I guess that all makes sense. But how does any of this tie back to a treasure?" She frowned. "I thought there was supposed to be a treasure somewhere in the mix."

"There may or may not be a treasure, which may or may not be related to what occurred at the theater," Mike confirmed. "Determining whether the gold, assuming it even exists, plays a role in the story is challenging, but we're still working to understand its significance. At this point, I'm operating under the assumption that twenty-four years ago, someone with a personal grudge against Gavigan O'Leary stabbed him twelve times behind the screen of the local movie theater after the movie ended and the place had emptied out. O'Leary's body was found, but the murder weapon never was. At the time, it was assumed that the killer took the murder weapon with him, but if the knife Tess found today ends up being the murder weapon, then it seems likely that the killer dropped the knife and it slid under the opening at the bottom of the fake interior wall. The killer couldn't reach it, so he left it. Jake somehow learned about the knife and went to look for it. He was shot in the head, presumably by O'Leary's killer, before he could find it."

"And how did Jake find out about the knife in the first place?" Bree asked.

Tony responded this time. "We think the killer told him." He went on to explain about the podcast dedicated to O'Leary's violent death and the comments that were left after the podcast was aired. Tony assured her that he planned to try to weed through all the comments but hadn't been home at all today, so he'd have to tackle that question tomorrow.

"I guess that all makes sense," Bree said. "I'm still not sure how the gold fits in, but otherwise, I feel as though I'm up to date."

"The gold was discussed in a podcast aired to a select audience on the dark web," I said. "The murder at the theater and the clues that were revealed relating to that murder were broadcast to the public at large on a mainstream platform. I know it seems that since Jake discussed both the murder and the gold during the same period, they must be related, but that isn't necessarily true. It's possible for a hard-core conspiracy theorist to be working on two completely unrelated conspiracy theories simultaneously."

"I guess that's true," Bree acknowledged.

"Garlic or no garlic on the bread?" Tony asked.

"No garlic," Bree and I said at the same time. I loved garlic, but Tommi definitely did not. Based on Bree's reply, I suspected Michael wasn't a fan either.

Tony set the food on the table, and Bree commented about hoping that Michael slept through the meal so she could enjoy it.

"Speaking of sleeping babies, where is Ella?" I asked. "I just realized she isn't here, and it's late for a nap."

"Your dad and Sam took her fishing."

"Fishing?" I asked.

Bree nodded. "I know that sounds like a bad idea, but Mike insisted that it would be fine, and I really did need to get some rest today while Mike was at work, so I agreed. Initially, I hoped your mom would go along, but she had to work, so it is just the two grandpas."

I glanced out the window. It was almost dark. "Shouldn't they be back by now?"

Bree glanced at the window, but it was Mike who replied. "Dad texted a while ago and said he and Sam were on their way home. He promised to be here by seven."

I glanced at the clock. It was six forty-three. I hoped the men were on time so Bree didn't start to worry. I felt that Ella, who was only three, was much too young to enjoy fishing. I hoped she hadn't had a truly miserable day.

"It looks like they're here," Mike said as headlights in the driveway reflected off the window. He got up to open the door and greet the men. I wasn't sure what I was expecting, but the grin on Dad's face as he carried a totally filthy child who was fast asleep on his shoulder almost had me in tears.

"She's going to need a bath," Dad said.

"She's totally out, so a bath may need to wait until tomorrow," Mike said. "Did you all have fun."

"The best time," Dad replied. "I'll carry her up to her room. One of her parents can get her into her pajamas. Then, once she's settled, I'll tell you all about it." He took a deep breath. "Do I smell marinara?"

"There's plenty if you're hungry," Tony offered.

Sam commented about needing to get home, but Dad responded to Tony's offer by telling him he'd love some once he dropped Ella off in her room.

Bree and I followed Dad upstairs. Ella tightened her grip around his neck when he leaned over to lay her on her mattress.

"Dapa," she said, clinging to him with all her strength.

"We're home now, angel. Mommy is going to put your jammies on."

"Don't go," she said as she began crying.

He kissed her forehead. "I'll come back in a day or two so we can play some more. I promise. But now, I need you to be a good girl for your mommy."

Ella kissed my dad on the cheek before letting go of him. Based on the display I'd just witnessed, Ella had experienced an exceptional day.

Michael began to fuss before Bree finished with Ella, so I offered to take over with the older child.

"Did you have fun today?' I asked Ella as I used a warm washcloth to clean the first layer of dirt from her face, arms, hands, feet, and legs.

"I got a fish." She wrinkled her nose. "I didn't want to hurt it, so Dapa put it back in the water."

"That sounds like quite the adventure."

"What venture?"

"Fun time," I simplified. I guessed I needed to brush up on my toddler talk. Ella actually had an impressive vocabulary for a three-year-old, but there were still rarely used words she didn't recognize.

Ella's eyes were half-mast by the time I'd washed her and put her pajamas on. I kissed her on the cheek, checked her nightlight, turned off her light, and joined the men downstairs. Dad was eating Tony's pasta and drinking a beer as he shared photos of his day. Given Ella's wide grin in every single photo, it definitely appeared that she'd had a wonderful time. Who knew that Ella had taken after her daddy when it came to her love of the great outdoors. Or perhaps the affection of her two doting grandpas was responsible for the joy in her eyes.

Chapter 16

By the time Wednesday rolled around, Tim and Tom had filmed dozens of hours of footage. Both men assured us that at least two ghosts haunted the old theater. I assumed it must be Gavigan O'Leary and Jake Black, but Tony informed me that Tim and Tom thought that one of the ghosts had been there since before O'Leary was stabbed to death. Tony wanted to head to the theater and check in with the men, so I decided Tilly and I would go into town. I wanted to check in with Bree and the kids, and it had been forever since I'd visited with Mom. I figured Mom would be at work this morning, so I decided to start there and then visit with Bree later in the morning. When I arrived at the restaurant Mom and Aunt Ruthie owned together, the place was dead except for two women sitting at the counter talking with Ruthie.

"Tess," Mom greeted. "How are you, sweetheart?"

"I'm feeling pretty good today. I seem to be past the fatigue and morning sickness, which is nice."

"I remember that the seventh and eighth months weren't too bad. Can I get you some decaf coffee or herbal tea?"

"Some herbal tea would be nice."

Mom brought me my tea and joined me in a corner booth in the back. Tilly knew she needed to wait quietly under the table when visiting the restaurant, so she settled in and waited for someone to reward her with a cookie. As she always did, Mom came through.

"I was at Mike and Bree's house when Hank and Sam brought Ella home after fishing," I said in a hushed tone, careful to avoid drawing attention to our conversation. The women at the counter were laughing and talking loudly, so I didn't think they were paying a bit of attention to us, but still, I knew to be careful about what I said in a public place. "At first, I was doubtful about the plan to take her fishing, but she seemed to have fun."

"I spoke with Sam about it after they got home. He said that Ella had a blast. He also said that if someone asked him to venture a guess, he'd say he thought she might lean towards being a bit of a tomboy."

"Tony and I were talking about our baby, and we think she'll probably be a tomboy. Not that we really have any way of knowing what sort of activities she'll prefer, but I was a tomboy, so I guess it's the little girl who loves to fish and play baseball that I can imagine over one who prefers tea parties and dolls."

"While it is true that you never had dolls, you did have a room full of stuffed animals, and you used to have tea parties with them when you were around four or five."

"I did?" I honestly didn't remember that.

"I have a photo of one of your tea parties. You set at least a dozen stuffed animals up around that little round table in your bedroom, and then somehow, you managed to convince your dad to join you and your friends for milk and cookies. You wore a crown that had come with your Halloween outfit, and you made your dad wear a flower in his hair from the bouquet in the kitchen. It was adorable."

"Dad wore a flower in his hair?" I laughed.

She nodded. "Your dad tucked it behind his ear."

"I wish I could remember that, but I don't. Do you know where the photo is? I'd love to see it."

"It's in a box with a bunch of other photos from your childhood. I'll look for it when I have time."

I took a sip of my tea. "Is it weird for you to have Dad here, especially given that you've already moved on with Sam?"

Mom reminded me to refer to Hank as Hank and not anyone else while in public, and I promised I would try harder to remember.

"To answer your question, it was weird at first, and I guess, in a way, it still is. But Hank seems to be fine with Sam and me, and Sam seems to be fine with the fact that Hank is back in our lives, so I'm trying to maintain what I have while hanging onto my memories of the past and not letting my two lives explode into each other. While it's not always easy, it is essential, so I am committed to working on it daily. Ultimately, I think we'll all find a way to be a family and embrace our new normal."

I looked toward the counter. The women had left, and Ruthie had gone into the kitchen, so only Mom and I were in the dining room. I lowered my voice and asked a question that I couldn't seem to get out of my mind. "And you aren't tempted to pick things back up with Dad?"

She shook her head. "I'm really not. The years I had with your father are years I will always treasure. He's the father of my children and the grandfather of my grandchildren. He will always hold a special place in my heart, but things weren't perfect between us, and, to be honest, Sam and I are a better fit than your dad and I ever were. I've spent some time asking myself why he married me when he likely knew the entire time that he'd have to leave at some point. I'm not sure I'll ever know the answer to that question, but if you ask me, I think it's entirely possible that marrying and having a family was simply part of his cover at the time."

"You think so?" I asked.

"I think that it's at least a possibility. That doesn't mean that your dad didn't love me, and it certainly doesn't mean that he didn't love you kids, but I think the plan all along was to fake his death and disappear at some point."

I supposed Mom could be right. Dad had put his job above all else for many years but seemed genuine in his desire to retire and rejoin our lives at this point. I just hoped for all of us that turned out to be true.

"So, do you and Dad think you can be friends?" I asked. "Just friends."

"I know we can. We already are."

I supposed if Mom was okay with things the way they were, then I would stop worrying about the emotional trauma I really thought Dad would bring into Mom's life if he ever came home and returned to the life he left behind all those years ago.

"Have you thought any more about a shower?" Mom asked, changing the subject as a large group walked in, and Ruthie came out to greet them.

"No shower. Tony and I have everything we need. There's no need for a shower, and, honestly, I'm just not into it."

"Okay." Mom held up her hands in surrender. "I wanted to ask one last time in case you'd changed your mind since the last time we chatted about it."

"I haven't, and I won't."

"I guess I should get back to work. It looks as if the lunch crowd is a few minutes early today. Will you and Tony be attending the Halloween Festival activities this weekend?"

"We will. Let's plan to meet up at the food court at some point on Saturday."

"I'd like that. I'll text you later, and we'll firm up our plans."

After I left the diner, I walked across the street to Hap's hardware and home supply store. I hadn't necessarily planned to drop in on Hap, but since I'd been so close, I couldn't resist stopping by.

"Morning, Hap," I greeted as I entered his store through the front door.

"Tess, Tilly. What brings the two of you by?"

"We were across the street visiting with Mom and decided to stop in and say hi before we left."

"Well, I'm glad you did."

Hap offered Tilly a cookie as he always did, and I grabbed a piece of hard candy from the jar as I always did. There was something so perfect about the everyday routines that fill out your life and give it texture. Since giving up my mail route, I'd missed Hap and many of my regulars. Not that I was at that point in my life where I wanted that sort of daily responsibility, but there were moments when I longed for the comforts of its predictability.

"I heard Sam and his friend, Hank, took Ella fishing," Hap said."

"They did. Have you spoken to Sam?"

"He came in with Hank. Hattie rounded both men up to help with the Halloween Festival."

I raised a brow. "No kidding? What did she talk them into doing?"

"She has them setting up the booths for the kiddie carnival and the food vendors today. I'm sure that once that's finished, she'll find something else for them to do. Now that Hattie has decided to help take the burden off you and Tony, she's all in." Hap chuckled. "That woman I married is still as much of a spitfire as she was on the day I married her the first time."

Hap and Hattie had a unique relationship. They'd been married for quite a few years but then divorced, although they continued to date. After trying out "single but dating" for a while, they decided to remarry in a private ceremony.

"Tony and I appreciate everything Hattie is doing. What do you think of Sam's friend, Hank?"

I knew this was a risky question, but Hap had known my dad when he'd lived in White Eagle as Grant Thomas, as well as anyone had. I supposed I would actually begin to believe that Dad would get away with his reentry into White Eagle society as a completely different person if Hap didn't suspect that Hank and Grant were the same person.

"I like him. He seems to be a good guy who is happy with the simple things in life. He likes to do a lot of the same things I like to do, and in addition to our white hair, we seemed to have a lot in common. Based on our brief discussion when he came in with Sam, he seemed happy to do his part around town. I think the two of us are going to get on just fine. In fact, meeting the guy was almost like meeting up with an old friend rather than getting to know someone for the first time."

I smiled. "I'm glad the two of you hit it off. I'm still getting to know Hank, but like what I've seen so far."

Hap and I chatted a little longer about nothing in particular, just as we had hundreds of times. After leaving Hap's store, I felt much better about Dad and his reentry into my world. If Dad managed to spend time with Hap and Ruthie without being recognized, I'd consider us safe.

I was planning to head back to my vehicle that I'd parked behind Mom's restaurant when I noticed Tony's truck parked on the street in front of Mike's office. Changing direction, I headed that way.

"Hey, guys, is something up?" I inquired, approaching Mike, Tony, Frank, and Gage, who were gathered around the rectangular conference table.

"I stopped by to tell Mike about the ghost Tim and Tom have been interacting with. The ghost seems stuck due to unresolved issues relating to a relationship that went wrong," Tony said. "It sounded like the ghost might have been O'Leary, so I figured I'd pass the tip along."

"Do you think that's what happened?" I asked. "Did O'Leary have a girlfriend after all?"

"Not exactly," Tony said.

Mike jumped in. "We got a hit on the fingerprint on the knife you found at the theater."

"Whose fingerprint?" I asked as I waddled a bit closer with Tilly on my heels.

"Glen Price," Tony said.

It took me a minute to remember where I'd heard that name. "Glen Price is the guy Shaggy knew who also knew Gavigan O'Leary and Jake Black."

Tony nodded.

"I thought you cleared him."

Tony responded. "I won't go so far as to say that I cleared him. I did talk to him, and he didn't say anything that would indicate that he had anything to do with the death of either man. The only thing we really had on him was that he seemed to have known both men. Given the gap between the murders, there weren't a lot of people who still lived in town who would have had reason to know both men, but I'm sure there were others."

"So if the fingerprint found on the knife we suspect to have been the murder weapon in the O'Leary stabbing do belong to Price, then he likely killed the man," I said.

Mike, who had been leaning over documents on the table since I'd first walked in, straightened. "That would seem to be the case. We still need to match the blood on the knife to O'Leary to really make our case, but we have enough to bring Price in." He looked at Gage. "Frank and I will pick him up while you hold down the fort here."

With that, Mike and Frank left, leaving Gage, Tony, and me.

"How long does Mike think it will take to get a match for the blood on the knife?" I asked Gage.

"It's hard to say. The gap between now and when the blood likely first was deposited on the knife is significant. For us to arrest this guy, we'll likely need a confession."

"Any idea why Glen Price would have killed O'Leary?" I asked. I remembered that both men had worked at the theater at the same time, but that wasn't a reason in and of itself to kill a man.

Gage shrugged. "We've been kicking around some theories, but so far, we haven't come up with proof to support any of those theories."

"I haven't been around for all the conversations involving Glen Price," I said. "I remember that he worked in the snack bar at the theater when O'Leary worked there as an usher. I remember that Glen was a part-time employee and that while he was questioned at the time of O'Leary's murder, as were all employees, he claimed not to know anything."

"That much is right," Gage confirmed. "We also found a woman who worked part-time at the theater when O'Leary died, and she said that O'Leary and Price were close."

"How close?" I asked, remembering the tip Tony had relayed to Mike from Tim and Tom about a romance gone wrong.

"She indicated that there had been a rumor at the time that the men were *very* close," he emphasized the word very, "but she also said she'd never witnessed any intimate activity, and she had no proof of anything. What she'd heard, she'd heard through gossip."

"So O'Leary and Price might have been lovers?"

"If the rumor mill was correct. Again, this woman admitted that she had absolutely zero proof that the rumors were true."

"That may be," I said, "but most rumors are based on at least some degree of truth, and the ghost Tim and Tom have been chatting with mentioned a romance gone bad."

"If the men were involved and things went south, that would account for the rage that the killer must have felt to stab someone twelve times," Tony pointed out.

"Mike thought so as well," Gage informed us. "He's been digging into Price's life, but until the fingerprint was matched, we didn't have a smoking gun."

I took a moment to think this through. If Glen and his older coworker had been involved in a relationship of the intimate sort, and if for some reason O'Leary broke it off, that could have sent his young lover into a tailspin. O'Leary might even have been Price's first lover, or at least his first male lover. When the man Price went all in for broke it off, I could see how he might become enraged enough to do what he had.

"Okay," I said. "So Price kills O'Leary, but he drops the knife, and it slides under the wall. He either didn't notice where it ended up or he knew where it landed but couldn't reach it, so he leaves it there. He figures that no one will find it, and, as it turns out, it was a long time before someone did. And then Jake somehow comes up with a theory involving the missing knife. I don't think Jake knew where it was since he didn't seem to go right to it, but he knew that it had never been recovered, so he figured it was still in the theater. He makes noise on his podcast about going to the theater to look for it, so Price, who wants to be sure the knife is never found, shoots him and then shoves him into the control room. The old theater is locked up to prevent further vandalism, so Jake's body remains undiscovered until Tilly found it last week."

"That's the theory," Gage said. "We know that Price worked at the lumber mill with Jake, so Mike thinks it may even have been Price who let something slip that put the idea in Jake's mind to go after the knife in the first place."

"I can see how a few beers after work between friends could lead to that," Tony said. "The men had a lot in common. I'm sure a casual get-together between coworkers often led to a discussion about one conspiracy theory or another."

About fifteen minutes after Mike and Frank left to speak to Price, Mike called Gage and asked for backup. Apparently, Price had a gun and had barricaded himself in his house. Mike assured Gage that no one was hurt, but Price wasn't coming out, and he wasn't allowing anyone to approach the house. Mike wanted Gage to call the state police, inform them of the situation, and then head to Price's house with extra guns and ammunition. Of course, Tony and I were told to wait where we were for further instruction. I wanted to help, but there really wasn't anything I could do that wouldn't put Tommi in danger.

"You would think Price would know that the only way he's getting out of that house is in handcuffs or a body bag. I don't get the point of the standoff," I said to Tony after Gage left.

"Desperate people don't always think clearly. I'm sure the instinct to fight to the end is strong. Regrettably, situations like this often escalate, and the worst-case scenario frequently becomes the reality."

I could hear the sound of sirens in the distance. Mike and Frank were already on the scene, and Gage had left long enough ago that I wouldn't be hearing his siren. It must be the state police. I hoped that was true. The thought of Mike and his team having to take on this obviously unstable man alone was unsettling.

The standoff lasted six hours. My nerves were shot by the time Mike called to let us know that Price was in custody and that the state police were taking him to county holding. It had been a stressful day, but once the man gave up, he decided to confess to killing both Gavigan O'Leary and Jake Black. The story we'd come up with was pretty darn close to the truth, which should have landed us some level of satisfaction, but no matter how you looked at it, the story was nothing short of tragic.

Chapter 17

"Almost done," Tony said as we drove from town toward the Stonewall Estate on Saturday afternoon. It had been a long day that had started early with the community parade, followed by the kiddie carnival, where we cheered Ella on as she attempted some of the entry-level games. This was followed by a visit to the craft fair and then a late lunch in the park while we waited for the winners of the chili cookoff to be announced.

"I'm exhausted."

"I can run you home if you'd like. I don't want you and Tommi overdoing it."

"I think we already overdid it, but I want to be here for the big show. Maybe we can sneak out early."

"We'll plan on it."

The filming of *Ghost Therapy* at the Stonewall Estate was set to take place from six until eleven. The twenty-five auction and ten lottery winners were instructed to arrive by five. Tony and I had planned to be there by four, but it was already after four-thirty.

"Do you think they really have made a connection with the ghost of Buford Stonewall as they indicated they had?" I asked Tony.

He furrowed his brow. "My instinct is to say that the whole ghost thing is nothing more than an illusion created by the men to give authenticity to their show, but they did seem spot on about what was going on at the theater."

"It is weird that the men told you about the failed romance angle before Mike told you the identity of the individual who left the fingerprint on the knife. The fact that they turned out to be right almost makes me a believer."

"I suppose it might have been a ghost who shared the tip about the romance, or perhaps they had another way to figure out what actually happened."

"They could have been making the whole thing up and just happened to be right. A love affair gone bad as a motive for a killing involving twelve stab wounds isn't a bad guess."

"And it was a low-risk guess," Tony pointed out. "If the motive for O'Leary's death ended up being something other than a love affair gone bad, all they had to say was that the ghost they chatted with must have been referring to another love affair, one not related to O'Leary and his death."

"I guess the real test will be to see if the men come up with the hidden gold. If they actually chat with Buford Stonewall, then he should be able to tell them where to look."

"If there ever was any gold," Tony pointed out.

By the time Tony and I pulled up to the mansion, a crowd had already begun to gather.

"I need to track Jazzy down. Do you want to wait here?" Tony asked.

"Yes, I do. Things won't get interesting for another hour to ninety minutes, so I may as well reserve my strength."

Tony promised to return once he checked in with Jazzy and determined what, if anything, needed to be done. He had his cell phone, and I had mine, so he instructed me to call him if I needed anything. I knew Tony would have preferred that Tommi and I had waited for him at home tonight, and, in retrospect, maybe that might have been the better move to make. But I was pregnant, not an invalid, and since I would have a child to consider next October, this might very well be my last chance to experience a ghost therapy session.

By the time Tony returned to the truck, all thirty-five audience members had arrived, and two men with bright orange vests had begun to escort them inside. Since I didn't recognize the men, I assumed they were employees of the television station producing the show.

"Is everything on track?" I asked Tony.

"It seems to be. Tim and Tom, along with their crew, spent Thursday evening and all day Friday setting up, and they've also been here since early this morning, so I think they're ready to film. I asked Tim if he thought the ghost would show up with so many spectators around, and he said probably not. He also said they had filmed quite a few segments yesterday and during the overnight hours last night to use for the show. They have props set up to help make their session this evening believable so the men and women who paid to witness the therapy session won't leave disappointed."

"So Tim indicated that what they do is real and fake, both in the same sentence."

Tony laughed. "Yes, I guess he did." Tony looked out the window. The crowd was still entering the mansion. "I'm going to take the extension cord I have in the back of the truck to the crew. I'll return for you after I help them set up the additional lighting they seem to believe is necessary. Everyone should be inside when I return, and we can find a comfortable place to view the show. Will you be okay here alone for another fifteen or twenty minutes?"

"I'll be fine. Go and do what you need to do."

It was getting dark, but I had the interior lights I could turn on if I needed them. I also had a flashlight and the light from my cell phone. I wasn't the sort to be afraid of the dark, even if Tony was delayed, so I wasn't worried. It had been such a busy day that sitting helped to relieve some of the pressure I'd been experiencing in my back.

Tony had parked his truck in the same lot as the thirty-five ticket holders, so it didn't stand out. The other vehicles were empty, the sun had set, and the sky had darkened, so I wasn't surprised when two of the *Ghost Therapy* crew members decided to smoke a cigarette less than twenty feet from where I was sitting. I supposed I could have made some noise to let them know I could hear their conversation, but I was bored, so I decided to sit quietly and listen in. When the first man spoke, I realized immediately that while both men were wearing orange vests, the tall, dark-haired man was the same man I'd run into when Tony and I had come to check the place out. I was willing to bet the other individual was the second man to arrive as Tony and I prepared to leave the estate.

"We should have found it by now," the man whose voice I recognized said to the other man. I remembered that the man with the black cowboy hat had introduced himself as Lawrence Hightower, one of the Stonewall cousins.

"I agree, but there's no way we could have anticipated all the setbacks or the early arrival of the *Ghost Therapy* crew. Our best bet is to wait until they leave and pick up where we left off."

"What if the men establish a connection with a ghost, one who is aware of what's going on?" the first man asked. "What then?"

The second man laughed. "Don't tell me you actually believe all this ghost stuff."

"Don't tell me you don't."

I watched as a man came out of the mansion carrying a roll of cable. He headed toward a utility truck, which appeared to prompt the men I'd been eavesdropping on to walk away. I was evaluating the wisdom of leaving the truck's comfort to follow the men when I noticed Tony walking toward me. I supposed his arrival should have been considered good timing since even though I really wanted to figure out what was happening, I knew it wasn't just my life that I would be risking when I did crazy things. It was Tommi's life as well, which was a situation that I wanted to avoid at all costs.

"Do you remember the two men who showed up during our walk-through?" I asked.

"The cousins?"

I nodded. "Both men are here, and based on what I overheard, it's as though they're still looking for something. They seem determined to get it. In fact, one guy truly appeared worried that Tim and Tom might connect with a ghost who might share the location of whatever they're after with them. Of course, the second guy thought the first guy was nuts."

"I suppose the men could be looking for the gold. It's really the only thing that makes sense." Tony hesitated. "I'm not supposed to say anything, but I was talking to the cameraman I was helping just now, and he told me that Tim and Tom had been communicating with a ghost, but it wasn't Buford as they're telling everyone."

"Then who?" I asked.

"Josephine Bardot. Apparently, Josephine was Buford's mistress. She officially lived on the property as a tutor for Buford's children, but everyone knew that the master of the house and the tutor were sleeping together."

"And Buford's wife?"

"She was ill and basically bedridden for years before she finally passed. Shortly after she passed, the tutor left the property. Some say she moved for another assignment, but others say she met with foul play."

I took a moment to digest this. "So if Tim and Tom have made contact with Josephine, she should be able to tell them what really happened to her."

"I suppose she would," Tony agreed.

"The woman in the window," I said. "That must have been Josephine."

"If we suspend disbelief and choose to operate under the assumption that ghosts are real, then I suppose it would seem it that it was at least possible that the woman you saw in the window could have been Josephine's ghost. Of course, if the woman you saw was Josephine's ghost, then that seems to prove that she died here on the property, which means she hadn't simply left her employment to take another job."

"Do you think the men I overheard earlier know that it's Josephine Tim and Tom have been talking to?" I asked.

Tony shrugged. "Based on what has been said, I think it's more likely that the men found out about the gold and are afraid that Tim and Tom might have an inside track, which would help them to find it before they do."

"Do you think Tim and Tom are in danger? Those two men seemed determined to accomplish whatever they're here to accomplish."

"I don't think the men will do anything during the taping with so many witnesses hanging around, but it might not be a bad idea to warn Tim and Tom and to fill Mike in on what we suspect might happen. We can call Mike now, but we should wait to warn Tim and Tom until after the taping ends. I can run you home."

"I'm fine," I assured Tony.

"It's likely to be late by the time we make it home."

"It will be late, but not that late, and we can sleep in tomorrow. The taping is supposed to wrap up by eleven, and by that point, everyone will leave. We can talk to Tim and Tom and will be home by midnight."

Our plan seemed reasonable at the time we made it, but what we couldn't have predicted was the ghost who led us to the skeleton in the wall.

Chapter 18

"So the ghost of Buford's mistress somehow shared with Tim and Tom that she'd been murdered and her body had been entombed behind a wall in the attic," Shaggy said the following day. Tony and I had decided to thank him for all his help with the case by bringing him up to speed on the juicy details we'd been sworn to keep to ourselves and that very few people knew.

"That's the gist of it," Tony confirmed.

"And why was she murdered?" Shaggy asked.

"Josephine apparently suspected that Buford's best friend and money manager, Devon Burgman, had been siphoning off the gold coins Buford had brought with him when he came west. Josephine had never liked or trusted the man, so she began to snoop around. When he found her snooping, he killed her and then entombed her body behind a fake wall in the attic. Josephine has been haunting the house ever since."

"Did she know about the gold?" Shaggy asked. "Did she know where it was hidden?"

"She knew about the gold but didn't know where it was or if it still existed," Tony answered. "But she did say that Buford's son, Brandon, was a gambler who never seemed to have a dime to his name, so she assumes the gold was long gone before he died and passed the house on to his son."

As I sat and listened to the conversation between Shaggy and Tony, I tried to wrap my head around the fact that we were discussing the details of a conversation between a ghost and two men who claimed to be ghost therapists with complete sincerity. The whole thing was totally surreal, and if I hadn't seen a woman in the attic window myself, I likely would have suspected that Tim and Tom had made the whole thing up to lend authenticity to the series of shows they planned to air about their experience in the mansion. Of course, I didn't possess any proof that the woman I'd seen in the window was Josephine. The sun was setting when I'd seen her, and the light from the darkening sky could have been playing tricks on me. Or the woman could have been a very live woman who had come with one of the two men Tony and I had encountered. At this point, I supposed I might never know what had occurred that evening with any degree of certainty.

Mike and his team had been able to track down the men I'd overheard before the taping at the mansion and bring them in for questioning. Of course, all Mike had on them was my retelling of what I'd overheard, which wasn't enough to detain to hold them for long. At this point, we just hoped that now that the men knew the police were watching the estate, they'd move on.

"So, were Tim and Tom successful in helping Josephine to move on?" Shaggy asked after the conversation between Shaggy and Tony began to wind down.

"They said they were," Tony confirmed. "But not until Josephine led them to the proof needed to help her great-great-grandson."

"Great-great-grandson?" Shaggy asked. I could tell that even he was having difficulty believing all of this, and the truth of the matter was, all we really had was the word of the Ghost Therapists that they had actually chatted with Buford's mistress and that she had been the one to lead them to the bones. "I thought the woman died in the mansion while serving as both a tutor and mistress. How can she have a great-great-grandson?"

"This is the best part," I jumped into the conversation I'd only been observing up to this point. "Apparently, Josephine had a son. Buford's son. She secretly delivered him and gave him to her sister to raise. That was the only way Buford would agree to support and protect the child. That son had a son, and so on, and apparently, it's the great-great-grandson who has come forward and mucked up the claim of the Stonewall cousins by insisting that, as a direct descendant, he should be the one to inherit the Stonewall Estate, not them."

"But he wouldn't have proof," Shaggy pointed out.

"He didn't until Josephine led Tim and Tom to her son's original birth document, which was signed by both Buford and the midwife. The document still needs to be authenticated, but I thought it looked pretty real when Tim and Tom showed it to us."

"So it was the birth document and not the gold the men were after," Shaggy surmised.

"That does seem to be the case," Tony agreed.

Shaggy shook his head. "Talk about a crazy end to a crazy story."

"It really has been a very odd couple of days," I agreed.

Shaggy picked Tang up, and the pair settled into the thick cushions of the chair he'd been sitting on. I curled into a corner of the sofa as Tony pulled a blanket over my lap, and then Tilly and Tony settled onto either side. Shaggy mentioned a video game he thought we should try. While there had been a lot of changes in my life lately, the one thing that hadn't changed were nights spent with Shaggy and Tony and the video games that brought us together in the first place.

Christmas Eve

Christmas carols played softly in the background as gently falling snow coated the ground outside my window. The tree Tony had cut down and the two of us had decorated the night before Tommi decided to introduce herself to Tony and me twinkled with colored lights that seemed to reflect the flames from the nearby fireplace. I looked down at the sleeping baby in my arms as the scent of the evergreen tree filled the air. In this quiet moment, I felt a deep happiness and contentment that I couldn't remember feeling for quite some time.

"You need to head upstairs and get ready if you don't want to be late," Tony said after he entered the room from the rear of the house where he'd gone to grab more wood for the fireplace.

"I know," I smiled as Tommi made a face in her sleep. "But I'm so comfortable." I looked down at Tilly, lying at my side with her head in my lap. She adored Tommi and rarely left her side. If I held Tommi to comfort or nurse her, Tilly was there to lend support and comfort. "Tilly and I would like to request fifteen more minutes."

Tony dropped off the wood he'd brought in, careful not to disturb Titan and Kody, who were sleeping on the rug in front of the fireplace. "Fifteen more minutes, but then we really need to get moving. Your mother is expecting us."

I glanced out the window. "It's snowing. Maybe we can simply call and tell Mom we're snowed in."

"We could, but that would be a lie. Your mom would know it, and we'd know it." Tony crossed the room. He sat down on the arm of the sofa next to me. "Although, this is a pretty perfect moment," he said as Tinder crawled into his lap. Tang was curled up next to Tommi between my right hip and the arm of the sofa where Tony was sitting.

I looked into Tony's big brown eyes. Eyes he shared with his daughter, I might add. "We should have insisted on a quiet Christmas Eve. It has only been two weeks since I delivered. I could have found a way to guilt my mom into going along with a Christmas Eve at home."

Tony ran a finger down Tommi's cheek. "You could have, but you would have regretted it. Not only is this the first Christmas for both Tommi and Michael, but this is the first Christmas the entire family will spend together, which includes your mother and father."

Tony had a point. I had been looking forward to Christmas with the entire Thomas family. I knew that Bree had made homemade stockings for Michael and Tommi to hang on the fireplace next to the one she'd made for Ella when she was born.

"I suppose, however, that a new baby might be a good excuse to leave shortly after dinner," Tony suggested.

I smiled at the man I loved beyond all else. "Now, you're thinking. We'll see everyone again for Christmas dinner at Mike and Bree's tomorrow. I love that my entire family will be together, but I really want our little family to have the chance to establish our own Christmas traditions."

Tony kissed me on the top of the head. "We'll leave early, and we'll have tomorrow morning together with just us. I think we'll have time to establish our own routine."

Tang must have felt squished between Tony and me because he got up and walked across the room to lay with the dogs in front of the fireplace. Tinder followed Tang after only a minute, but Tilly had no intention of budging until Tommi budged. I hated to say it, but Tommi might have replaced me as the number one girl in Tilly's eyes.

Tony slipped down into the little spot Tang had vacated. Somehow, he managed to fit a hip between the armrest and my hip, but Tilly was pretty well set on my left side, so Tony wiggled around a bit and made do with the room he had. He wrapped his arms around mine, put his head on my shoulder, and stared at his daughter. "I can't remember the last time I was this content."

"I know what you mean," I said. "That's not to say that I've been unhappy or discontent up to this point, but there always seems to be something to worry about, a destination to travel to, and a task that needs to be attended to." I glanced at the large clock above the fireplace. "For the next eight minutes, I have nothing to do other than to sit here and enjoy my husband, my baby, my animals, and my beautiful home."

Tony wiggled around a bit more before settling. "I suppose it might not be the worst idea to call your mom and try to convince her that we have a blizzard up here on the mountain."

I smiled as I glanced out the window at the gently falling snow. "I thought you were bringing the lasagna."

"I am. I spent all day making it."

"And isn't the lasagna considered to be the main dish?"

"It is," he agreed.

"Then I guess we should go." I laid my head on his. "We'll eat, sing a carol or two, open a gift, drive home, and pick things up right here. Exactly here," I emphasized.

Tony reluctantly agreed.

Tony had already changed his clothes, so he took Tommi to her crib while he gathered the baby supplies. Once he brought Tommi back downstairs, he let the dogs out and began to load everyone into the truck. I wasn't sure that taking all three dogs was the best idea, but it was Christmas Eve, and I didn't want to leave them home alone. Tony helped Tilly climb up on the back seat next to Tommi's car seat while Titan and Kody jumped up into the bed of the truck. Tony had put the shell on the bed and had tossed in an old mattress when we'd had our first snow so the dogs had a dry and comfortable place to travel.

"I've been thinking about Christmases from my past this week. Christmases when I was a kid and my dad was still around." I looked out at the white landscape. "I know we had some good ones, but we also had some not-so-good ones. Mom and Dad didn't always get along, which added tension to the situation." I turned and glanced directly at Tony. "Let's not do that. Let's not fight in front of our children."

"Never," he promised. "Do you have a favorite Christmas? Before this one, that is?"

"There have been a lot of really awesome Christmases since the two of us started spending Christmas together. The year you played Santa in the parade after my mother bit off more than she could chew with the Christmas Festival, and then there was the year when you rented the sleigh, and we went for a long ride through the woods. But I think my absolute favorite Christmas of all time, before this one, of course, is that first Christmas when you gave me proof that my father hadn't died when and how I'd thought he had. While that moment led to a lot of angst and heartbreak, it also led to a journey that would take us from friends to lovers to a happily wedded couple to proud parents."

Tony reached over and squeezed my hand. "And that journey is one I wouldn't have missed for the world."

The End

USA Today best-selling author Kathi Daley lives in beautiful Lake Tahoe with her husband Ken. When she isn't writing, she likes spending time hiking the miles of desolate trails surrounding her home. Find out more about her books at **www.kathidaley.com**

Made in the USA
Las Vegas, NV
17 November 2024

12023223R20115